AFTER THE FLOODS

After the Floods

• A NOVEL •

Review Copy — not for resale.

Bruce Henricksen

LOST HILLS BOOKS
DULUTH, MINNESOTA

© 2008 Bruce Henricksen
All rights reserved. Unless otherwise noted on a specific page, no portion of this publication may be reproduced or transmitted in any form or by any means, electronic or mechanical, including photocopying, recording, or capturing on any information storage and retrieval system, without permission in writing from the publisher, except by a reviewer, who may quote brief passages in a critical article or review to be printed in a magazine or newspaper, or electronically transmitted on radio, television, or the Internet.

Published by:
Lost Hills Books
P.O. Box 3054
Duluth, MN 55803
www.losthillsbooks.com

First edition 2008
Cover illustration: "Migrations," digital collage by Carla Stetson
Book design: Dorie McClelland, Spring Book Design
Cover design: Cathy Spengler, Cathy Spengler Design
Interior typeset in Adobe Garamond Pro and Adobe Myriad Pro
12 11 10 09 08   1 2 3 4 5
Manufactured in Canada

ISBN-13: 978-0-9798535-0-0
ISBN-10: 0-9798535-1-8

This book is dedicated to Paul and Thomas across the pond.
May your rivers be long and wide.

Contents

Children of the Wind   *1*

Birdie and the Phoenix   *23*

The Wanderers   *85*

Billy in the Shade   *99*

Branchings   *184*

River of Dreams   *199*

Acknowledgments

I've benefited from the help and encouragement of a number of people. As always, the captain of my dream team is my wife, Viki. Other players include Eileen Barrett, John Biguenet, Elizabeth Cleveland, Louis Jenkins, Paul Johnson, Jill Lyman, Dorie McClelland, Cathy Spengler, Carla Stetson, and Connie Wanek. Thanks, guys!

Children of the Wind

Ruby and George

It was May, but the heat had come early that summer, dripping
from trees and roof tops. Each afternoon, clouds from off the
Gulf of Mexico moved slowly toward the city, and each afternoon a gang of crows banked in the heavy air, swooped, and
latched on to the telephone line near the Nikes that dangled like
fruit. With cocking heads, they surveyed Laurel, a quiet resi-
dential street near the river. On this day, the Corvuses, perched
at a distance from the other crows, eyed a disheveled man in a
sweatshirt hunched on a rotting porch.

"He must be hot in that shirt," Ruby Corvus said.

"Termites," George said. "Lots of termites in that porch."

"Yum!" Ruby said agreeably. If the man in the sweatshirt
would scram, maybe they'd glide down and peck around.

Across the street from the porch, a dog sniffed a trash pile
and a ginger cat lounged on a table behind a cracked window.
All along Laurel, shutters hung at various angles like damaged
wings. A few air conditioners, jutting from the sides of houses
and tilting downward, clattered and sweated. Mostly, it was a
street of broken things, but the Corvuses visited there often.
Laurel is the street where Ruby's heart had been broken, broken
with the branch that snapped in the storm, sending her eggs
splattering to the sidewalk.

After the Floods

"Sometimes I hear voices in my feet. It's so odd," Ruby said, glancing at George.

"It's the wire. They talk through wires." George was proud of his knowledge.

"I had forgotten," Ruby replied. "I hear crying now . . . in my feet." She remembered seeing, as the flood subsided, dead things in puddles like huge tears.

"Yes," George replied. "I hear it too."

The street below had been picked over by dogs, cats, and people. In a few minutes, the boss crow barked orders from the far end of the phone line. "We ain't sitting here all day like clothes pins! Shake loose! We're heading for the dumpster behind the SuperValu."

"That's one crow who bugs me," George said. "Thinks he's top dog." They watched the others explode into the sky and become a shadow shattered against the distant clouds. "Everyone follows the herd," George mused. He jabbed his beak under a wing where a flea, freshly awake from an anxious sleep, had taken a bite.

"We fly to our own drummer," Ruby replied proudly. "We don't need that crowd."

She shuffled closer to George on the wire, feeling the strength of his wing against hers. She enjoyed such moments of togetherness, just the two of them against the world. Maybe she'd write a song about it. Ruby wanted to sing, although the skill eluded her.

The air smelled wet and green. Even though visiting Laurel Street was a little like visiting a cemetery, Ruby Corvus was happy.

Children of the Wind

Kyle and Andy

It was late in the afternoon, and the clouds were upon the city. On the porch, Kyle ate a Butterfinger and contemplated the dog across the street, a dusty, indeterminate creature of gray and brown who might have been swept together with a broom. Maybe that's where strays come from, Kyle thought. In the evening you sweep the dirt and debris out the door and into a pile on the porch, and then the night's voodoo turns it into another stray dog. It was a theory. Each day provided new dogs to contemplate, and watching the dogs kept Kyle's mind from sliding backwards into mist that was as gray as an old woman's hair.

Everything was clear back to Katrina, but before the hurricane it was all mist. He was certain he hadn't lived in New Orleans all his life, but his memory held no place to go back to. The picture on his driver's license was of him, but the address was unfamiliar. He had inquired where the street was, and when he found it in the Ninth Ward, on the far side of town, he faced a demolished house on a demolished block. It would have been barely recognizable even to a person with a memory, and in his mind nothing lay beyond the demolition site that he could call a past. No childhood, no parents, no town, no school. Just mist.

New Orleans had weakened progressively, as damage spread from the levee through the neighborhoods, from physical structures to social and economic structures, and from bodies to minds. It had been a cascade, as when a body shuts down one organ at a time. In Kyle's case, he couldn't remember how he had come to his present address, a shotgun house in a quiet neighborhood near the Irish Channel. Perhaps he had waded or paddled through snake-infested streets after the storm. Maybe

After the Floods

he had spent a night or two with the armies of lost souls in the Super Dome or the Convention Center. On the other hand, his car had apparently arrived with him to Laurel Street. It was all a mystery.

The crack on the bedroom ceiling of his present house slithered like a snake through a water spot. Kyle stared at it at night, hunting for his past. Then, in a dream, someone in robes would open a book of blank pages and read to him his crime. He would scream. It was better to sit on the porch than to go inside and face the crack. There was no telling what things might come through the crack at night.

"Yeah, you scream too much, you wild thing." The familiar voice was at once taunting and gentle.

Kyle turned to see, as he knew he would, Andy sitting on his haunches on the far end of the porch. His ponytail, which was knotted tightly at his head, hung to the middle of his back like Spanish moss. He'd come unannounced, letting Kyle know he'd been thinking aloud.

"People will say you're crazy," Andy said, "talking to yourself like that." He clutched a bone and gnawed it from time to time. The afternoon itself was a broken levee, and Kyle and Andy watched the evening and the rain that had started to flow through the yards and down the street.

Andy had told Kyle that he was born in a shack on a bayou north of Baton Rouge, where his parents lived the feral lives of meth heads. He remembered his mother picking at her flesh and screaming about bugs under her skin. She was just skin over bone, and her eyes were dark pits. When Andy was twelve, his dad shoved ten dollars in his pocket and told him to start walking. Andy had a ponytail even then.

Children of the Wind

"We're done. You're out of the nest," were his father's parting words. Andy gazed at the man's grin and his rotten teeth, and then he was swept out into the night.

Always in long-sleeved shirts now to hide the cuts, Andy showed up evenings on Kyle's porch, where the two would brood as darkness rose like water between houses. They'd brood as many people have done who travel back to an address scrawled on an envelope or in the mind, only to wonder, as in Matthew, before an empty tomb.

After dark Kyle and Andy would hunch over a chess board in the kitchen. Kyle usually lost, thanks to Andy's incessant chatter about beheading his parents and burning their shack.

"We could video tape it!" Andy said the other night. "Slaughter those pigs and croak it on the Internet!"

Animal sounds had found their way into people's vocabularies since the storm, and apparently *croak*, at least for the moment, meant "show" in Andy's mind. Kyle took the animal words for granted, but the talk about beheading made him uneasy, and he replied that, for his part, he just wanted to be left alone. He didn't need a past. Then he thought about how each life begins merely as an extension of the parents' lives, of their mistakes, delusions, successes, and so on. Slowly, over many years, a person's life becomes his own. Or doesn't.

Later, Kyle and Andy tumbled (because of the beer or the bourbon they always tumbled) into bed together. Andy couldn't be left alone.

"Let's do spoons," Andy always said, slipping close behind Kyle, his breath a moist veil on Kyle's neck. "*Moo*," Andy sighed.

After the Floods

A Meeting of Dogs

Kyle and Andy slept through the occasional gunfire from the street, but in the quiet hours, even when pressed close against Kyle, Andy often awoke screaming, just as Kyle did when Andy was away. Then Andy would slip from the bed like a snake from a log, and soon Kyle would find him in the kitchen with a carving knife poised above an arm or leg. Amidst shouting and stumbling, Kyle would wrestle the knife away.

In the morning there'd be blood on the sheets, but Andy was gone. Kyle would wash the knife as, perhaps, a roach cowered under the toaster. Then he'd prepare breakfast—sunny-side eggs, instant grits, and a biscuit. As he ate, in moments when the outside world was quiet, he'd hear the soft munching of a fly feeding by the sink in the ramshackle village of yesterday's dishes.

Then Kyle might drive to the levee, parking in the Riverbend lot by the Baskin Robbins and then walking toward Ochsner Clinic. The dog across the street from Kyle's house rarely spoke, but on the levee, unless there was jogger infestation, Kyle and his fuzzy friends chewed the fat. "Chew the fat" was what an old German shepherd called it. Kyle said the expression was way retro, but Adolph protested that Kyle had a poor feel for canine culture.

"Chew that fat is a popular expression these days," Adolph insisted, scratching his chin with a back paw, "because there's so little food. It helps a dog pretend that he's nourished."

After that, Kyle brought what food he could, always a bag of Tiny Tots the Jerky Treat for Dogs and sometimes bones and other scraps. Also a ball. There was usually a dog or two ready for a ball game, and one mutt, who was excessively proud of his few drops of border collie blood, criticized Kyle's weak throwing arm.

"Come on, pussy, make me run!" Bingo shouted over his

Children of the Wind

shoulder as he bounded down the bank of the levee toward River Road.

After the ball game, Kyle sprawled on the levee facing the Mississippi, and the dogs gathered about as the cellophane of the biscuit bag crackled or the scraps in the coffee can tumbled into the grass. Someone would say that it was time to pig out, and the Doberman always joked about being dog tired. Willy, a restless beagle, might go to sniff a dead crow or perhaps a dead rat washed up from the river, but most of the dogs just spread themselves out in the grass. Sometimes a ship drifted by, or a vee of ducks followed the river, seemingly slowed by the heavy gulf air. It was a tranquil time.

"Like they're swimming in chicken fat," one dog remarked, gazing off at the formation in the sky.

"Ever eat duck?" a black dog named Coal asked.

"Never cared for it," Adolph said. "Now chicken, that's a horse of a different color."

"I ate drowned horse once," an old terrier said, "not all by myself, but me and some others. Hard times, those were."

"They's all hard, the times is. They's all hard," Gertrude mused. She was a bitch of many sorrows and fleas. Her gas issues prompted the old terrier to joke about butt burping.

"Some say we couldn't talk before the storm," Coal said, eying Kyle. "They say our brains were not evolved. Anything to that?"

"I don't know," Kyle said. "I don't remember before the storm. The storm blew the past away."

"Hmmm," Coal grunted, annoyed at how difficult it had become to get straight answers.

Kyle had told the dogs about Andy, and sometimes one of them asked how Andy was doing. The dogs were polite, although, like Kyle, their memories were not the best, especially in regard to

9

After the Floods

human matters. When Kyle eventually excused himself, it was to go home and meet Andy.

"Home," Coal mused, watching Kyle angle down the side of the levee toward the Riverbend shopping area. "I wonder what home is." He always intended to ask, but each time he forgot and then Kyle was gone.

Often the dogs spoke among themselves about the new phenomenon of thought. At first they had experienced thoughts as irritants brought by the storm, irritants like disembodied fleas, fleas of the mind, but eventually they became comfortable with thought. Thoughts became *their* thoughts, small mental pets to be proud of. Finally, their thoughts became a part of them, and they found ways to describe things they had seen.

Coal had seen Lake Pontchartrain once, and he told how it had stretched across the horizon like an endless slab of marble. Gertrude said the sunset looked like bugs after you stomp on them, and another dog claimed to have seen the wine-dark sea.

"I don't know much about rivers," the old terrier said, "but I think this river is a large, gray worm."

Eventually, their conversations turned to such issues as free will, the nature of gravity, and the best forms of governance. One dog became a worshiper of a postulated supernatural dog who ruled everything from a mansion of many doggy beds. Another dog claimed expertise in the mating habits of spiders, and Adolph came to know all there was to know about delusional disorder among Persian cats. And so it went.

Children of the Wind

Busted

With Kyle at the wheel, the old Mustang prowled the littered streets in the afternoon so that Andy could sniff out new places to hunt. Andy carried a small spiral notebook and jotted down addresses of houses where women or the elderly lived alone, or houses where the occupants had evacuated. He also noticed people walking alone. There were many hunting grounds in the city, and Andy was wise enough not to limit himself to one area. In the middle of the afternoon, Kyle might stop for a shrimp or oyster po-boy to go, which he'd share with Andy in the car. Except for smoky bars in the small hours, Andy didn't enter public places with Kyle.

Kyle tried not to think about the specifics of Andy's hunting trips, pretending instead that the preliminary site visits were just a game. Andy's hunting occurred at night when Kyle slept. In the morning, despite the blood on the sheets, Andy would be gone and Kyle would find cash and often jewelry on the kitchen table.

At other times, after darkness had risen from gutters to fill streets, rooms, and then the sky, Kyle prowled the bars—Igor's, Cooter Brown's, and finally the Maple Leaf on Oak Street, where he'd find Kat. Once, a couple of months ago, she had dragged Kyle home in the pre-dawn blur, and she was still friendly, prancing along the bar in her Daisy Dukes and hooker boots.

"Is it warm in here," Kyle asked, "or is it you?"

"Kyle, you old hound," she replied, "don't think you're gonna sniff around this yard again." She warmed the warning with a smile. "Beer?" Her voice was a soft thing dressed in fur.

He nodded, and Kat slid him a bottle of Coors. Often she'd forget to collect, and as the evening tilted and swayed Andy

After the Floods

might materialize on the next stool, his face coming and going through the layers of smoke like the moon on a night of racing clouds. Then Andy would explain one of his theories, which Kyle called conundrunks.

Andy believed, for instance, that all physical objects are recording devices. When sound waves hit a wall, when they hit anything, they alter the vibration of the molecules and, according to the law of conservation, the molecules will never again vibrate in exactly the way they would if the sound hadn't happened. So if one had a device sensitive enough, one could hear conversations of the distant past as they still linger, let's say, in the walls of old shacks north of Baton Rouge.

Kyle knew that Andy's theories must have flaws, but in the beery light of the Maple Leaf, with Andy's head ducking and nodding, his ponytail swishing from side to side, and his fingers in motion like antennae, Kyle had trouble locating the flaws.

Sometimes their arguments grew loud and Andy's usual purr (like an engine, Kyle thought) turned to a screech of insults. "You're just a shadow," Kyle shouted in response. "You aren't real." At these times Kyle noticed people, grouped in separate packs, turning to look, showing teeth as they laughed or shook menacing heads in disgust. Then Kat would glide down the bar and smile.

"Take hold, dude," she'd say. "Talk to me a while."

Later, finding the sidewalk uneven, he'd careen toward his car, jab the keys at the ignition switch, and finally move off down Oak Street, drifting through stop signs and eventually bumping up onto the curb before his shotgun house on Laurel Street. Andy might still be gazing at him from the passenger seat, or he may have vanished into his own night's voodoo, becoming a ghost, a jackal, or a vampire.

• • •

Children of the Wind

One day as August boiled on, nearly a year after the storm, the police took Kyle away. Standing on his porch with the crows kibitzing from the wire, they cuffed his hands behind his back. There were no handles on the inside of the car's doors, and the rear seat was like a cage.

Fortunately for Kyle, each cell in Central Lockup was jammed with a mix of the vicious, the desperate, or the confused, so the police convinced the owners of Kyle's house not to press charges. In fact, Kyle had taken good care of the place and had even brushed green paint on the front door to match his Mustang, but the owners of the Laurel Street house had returned to New Orleans and wanted him out.

"You can't just move into someone's house like a crow in the strawberry patch," an officer told him in an interview room where there was no air conditioning and even the walls sweated. The officer's voice bounced like a ball, and he panted in the heat. "You're stuff is on the curb. You can go back there now, load your car, and drive away. We'll even take you back—no charge. After that, we don't want to see you in that neighborhood. Understood?"

He leaned across the table, his massive face compressing his neck into a series of ripples that fell in a mudslide into his collar. He was a giant Shar-Pei gazing into Kyle's eyes, wanting to be petted.

"Yes," Kyle said. He wore a Saints sweatshirt and his face dripped.

"You have some cash and a car," the officer said. "That's good. You can hole-up in your car until you find a place. But there aren't many jobs around here. You should think about going home. What's the story on your home?"

"I can't remember. I don't have a story."

"Then maybe you should think about going someplace else."

13

After the Floods

"Yes," Kyle said. "I have thought about someplace else."

"Well, good," the officer said. "I hear it's good hunting in Tampa. There's employment, and the girl's have those expensive Florida bouncers. You'd like Tampa."

"Maybe Tampa," Kyle said.

The officer cocked his head and looked expectantly at Kyle. "Got a biscuit?" he asked. "Maybe a Tiny Tot?"

"The Jerky Treat for Dogs?"

A Brief New Life

Kyle parked his Mustang by his stuff on the curb, or by what stuff the scavengers had left him, and motioned to the dog across the street. The dog, who said his name was Smoky, saw a chance to poke his head out of a car window and sniff the wider world, so he scrambled into the back seat. There were no crows on the line at that time.

"Tootles," Kyle said, glancing back at the house as the car pulled away.

The following day Kyle paid for a month in a small apartment on Dublin Avenue near the Maple Leaf Bar. It was a camelback house with flaking orange paint, Sponge Bob orange, and a front yard no larger than a box top. The stairs to the upper room were bolted to the side of the building and wobbled unpleasantly. The wrought iron steps were nearly a deal breaker for Smoky.

"Definitely unsafe," Smoky protested. "I want something solid under my feet. I have issues with seeing through the freaking steps. My paws will get trapped. I'll break a leg." Smoky retained an evolutionary memory of leg-hold traps.

Children of the Wind

But there were trade-offs at the new address, and Smoky got used to it. From the top landing, he and Kyle could look eye-to-eye with the crows in the oaks and on the wires. The steps would protect them from predators, and Smoky could look down and feel superior to the mutts holding hobo meetings in the shade of a tree in the neighbor's yard. The skinny whippet who ranted about sin and damnation was especially irritating. Also, Smoky enjoyed the many food smells and animal smells that swirled in the air by the landing. *I have an apartment*, Smoky thought. *Cool.*

Kyle went after Kat. She did not like the man she lived with, Bernard, now that she knew him, so she was juicy and ripe for the picking. She had discovered snakes under the insulation in Bernard's attic after hearing them murmur in the night above the ceiling. Snakes were everywhere in New Orleans, but she did not intend to live with them. Not the kind that murmured. She had standards. She drew lines. And besides, the world is full of Bernards.

So after minimal coaxing on a slow night, with only a few people in the Maple Leaf looking as though they'd crawled from the same shipwreck, Kat agreed to nest with Kyle and Smoky in the rafters of the camelback, explaining to Kyle that it would only be temporary. She was twenty-eight and couldn't be the slut behind the bar forever. It was time to move forward.

"I'm molting," she said with a grin as she rinsed glasses.

In view of their past, it didn't seem right to live with Kyle and deny benefits, but she made it clear that it was temporary. She'd find a better life. Maybe if she flew to Los Angeles . . . Her eyes grew misty as she sipped a beer and gazed at the window as though she could see the lack of light beyond.

She also insisted that Kyle not talk to Andy.

After the Floods

"It's just too weird," she said. "And no knives. Your arms are a mess."

Kyle wore a long-sleeved shirt, but Kat was right.

"I haven't seen Andy for a while," he replied, peeling the label from his beer. "Maybe he went back to Baton Rouge . . . or into the mist." His eyes also took on a distant look. Outside, the sidewalk tilted and heaved as a drinker wandered into the night.

"You should just go to Baton Rouge," she said. "You should face the demons."

• • •

But one day in early September, after Kyle had left the Leaf in a blur at 3 a.m. and Kat had stayed to finish her shift, he awoke in the afternoon to find a strange wallet, a wrist watch, and a Nokia cell phone on the kitchen table. The bloody knife was on the floor. Andy had been there. Kat was still asleep, and Kyle quickly hid the score and scrubbed the knife, hoping she had been too stoned to notice them on her way in that morning.

He left the apartment with Kat still sleeping and Smoky shoving a lump of Alpo around in a bowl with his nose. He picked his way carefully down the wobbling stair. On the ground, as a squirrel froze on the trunk of the neighbor's oak, Kyle was attacked by three men who slammed his head into the wall and then on the sidewalk, emptied his pockets, put a knife in him, and loped away like deer.

Kyle died in sunshine on the sidewalk, thinking of the potential lives he had wasted, the social overtures he'd rejected, the eyes he'd avoided, the phone calls he hadn't answered. All the lives he might have lived came like seeds in the wind and touched his face, only to swirl away as this one "real" life, always only a shadow of the other lives that might have taken root, quickly vanished.

Children of the Wind

George and Ruby Corvus watched the event from a telephone line, and a semi-transparent Andy, like a figure in a double exposure, watched from the top of the iron stairs. As Kyle died on the sidewalk, Andy dissolved into the afternoon air. The squirrel spiraled up the tree, thinking only of escape. The air smelled brown, and Ruby was not at her best.

"Ever eat on a human?" George asked.

"No, I'm all dumpsters and trash cans," Ruby replied, "occasionally road kill. You know that, George. You know I'm a trashetarian." She was irritated. She was having a bad feather day.

George couldn't remember sparrow droppings, as crows say, and sometimes he talked as though he and Ruby were strangers. It worried her that his memory was going, and she tried not to take it personally. Once, when she had mentioned a memory lapse, George had explained that each experience must wither and shrink before it fits into memory, and with a crow's skull being so small, well, many experiences simply wither into unrecognizable specks in their attempts to fit.

On the occasion of Kyle's death, George remained focused on the meal below. "It's a chance to move up," George suggested, "to put the trash can in perspective. I like to peck on a fresh eye." His voice was a coo embalmed in a cackle.

Some of their friends had already alighted on the ground near Kyle, stepping about and trying to get a feel for the situation.

"My feet grow sad when they hear the humans in the wires, the talking and crying. It doesn't seem right to eat on them when they die. Anyway, it would be upsetting to have your lunch wake up and smack you," Ruby said.

"Okay. Let's find a rat," George said. "Maybe if we fly over to the levee . . ."

The fat person who lived below Kyle and Kat waddled along

After the Floods

the sidewalk from Oak Street, carrying a new putty gun from the Ace Hardware. He had short legs, a small head on a long neck, and an oval body like a turtle's shell. He arrived just in time to shoo the crows on the ground, who had moved closer to the corpse, springing backward and forward, looking about nervously, and even risking a trial peck or two.

The man poked his cell phone and then went inside to find a sheet. The nails in the porch screamed a protest when he sat, and his small head withdrew a bit into his clothing. Smoky, sensing that his life was coming apart like a biscuit in water, whimpered behind the door upstairs and peed on the imitation Persian rug that Kat had brought from the house with the murmuring snakes.

In an hour, two grizzly policemen tumbled from a car, radioed for pickup, and then climbed the iron stair to recite questions at Kat. She informed them that she had no idea who would do such a thing. As they talked in the doorway, Smoky ducked out, braved the stairs with tentative paws, stopped to sniff the sheet and whisper goodbye, and then wandered along Dublin Avenue toward the river, sniffing trees and leaving graffito on a fence.

Back on solid ground and mopping their brows with hand-kerchiefs, the policemen growled at the man on the porch about the unsafe stairway. Eventually they understood that the man was not the property owner, and they decided to sit in the squad car under a tree with the AC on until the pickup crew arrived, which it did, wearing blood-proof gloves and hoisting the body that had been Kyle into a black plastic bag.

Later that day, hunched over yesterday's red beans and rice at the kitchen table, Kat calculated that the rent was paid for two more weeks. She had scooped up the diamond ring and some of the money from the table when she came in that morning. It wouldn't have much shelf life, and the police had taken what she

Children of the Wind

had left on the table "as evidence." She'd have to molt. She'd be born again, wiggling free of the old Kat cocoon.

A customer at the bar had asked her out, a professor from Tulane who tended toward jeans, sneakers, and French cigarettes. His name was Daryl, and the buzz proclaimed that he was divorcing. And he had kept his job through the post-Katrina layoffs. If she played her cards right . . . well, it could be a real Cinderella thing.

Smoky Moves On

George and Ruby landed in a cypress tree by the river and watched snakes curl about below, meowing in the mud. A purple sunset blossomed slowly to the west.

"I thought only kittens talked like that," Ruby said.

"That was way yesterday," George cackle-cooed. Despite the small skull, George often feigned great knowledge and even greater wisdom.

"The storm that changed everything," she mused. It would be a good title for a song, if she could remember it. Someday she would learn to sing.

"How can they live like that," George scoffed, still focused on the snakes, "slithering around in the mud. It's disgraceful."

"Maybe they'll evolve," Ruby said. "Anyway, it's a free country." Then, after a moment of thought, she suggested that they go to Minnesota. George needed a change.

"*Caw* Minnesota?" George asked.

"It's the happening new place," Ruby said. "There's this town called Cold Beak . . ."

"Cold, just what my beak needs!" George replied sarcastically.

After the Floods

Ruby shrugged her wings. Why Cold Beak, indeed? But George definitely needed a change. Strange new sounds were crawling about in his speech.

• • •

Smoky climbed the levee not far from the two crows and discovered an alligator dozing on the grassy side that faced the river. The gator was as solid and oblivious as stone. The dog ambled away, keeping his nose to the ground, and then made a circle of himself in the grass, where he rested like an old tire, vaguely trying to remember where he'd been.

My life is a circle, too, he thought. Images of a man, and of iron stairs that grabbed your paws, drifted behind his eyes and then darted away like minnows, leaving his mind clear. An old bag-lady of a dog showed up, said her name was Gertrude, and complained about the hard times.

"What's your name?" she asked.

"I can't remember for sure," Smoky said. "I think it's Smoky."

"You should wear a dog tag," Gertrude said, "as a reminder."

Smoky wasn't looking for a relationship, and he definitely wasn't interested in old bitches with arthritic hips. Nonetheless, out of politeness, he stood, walked behind her, and sniffed. *Yikes*, he thought.

Gertrude limped away, and soon Smoky headed back in the direction he had come. Seeing the still, corrugated trunk and the curled tail, Smoky wondered if alligators could talk and what a gator, who will stuff a dog under water for a week before eating him, what such a thing would have to say for itself. But he stayed wide of the dozing reptile. You let sleeping alligators lie.

Smoky wanted to go home, but he suspected that he was not doing so. He tried to think of how there could be a home

Children of the Wind

and then not a home. There were still things to learn. Perhaps he should go to Baton Rouge. The man, whose name came and went, had talked of Baton Rouge, but Smoky didn't know what direction it was in. Besides, that name, too, was fading fast in his mind. Baton Rou . . . Bat . . . and then it was gone.

Now, as he moved away from the alligator, he knew of no place to go and had nothing to anticipate. There were many *directions* for a dog to go, and he was taking one of them. But there were no *places* to go as the daylight leaked away. *Like water from a cracked bowl,* Smoky thought. *Everything leaks away.* He watched the river and wondered how it could forever move but also always be there, with its small places rising and falling, with its lips lapping the shore. Food smells came from dumpsters further off, and then it began to rain along the river.

• • •

I've lived my whole life in New Orleans, Ruby thought as she watched Smokey wander away. *I lost my eggs here, in the storm. It would be sad to leave, even if things are out of balance now. It's still a city where April nights smell of honeysuckle. And October is wonderful, too, after the summer heat. The houses with wrought iron balconies make me think of those lovers from Verona, and of the old nights when George and I cuddled in branches and talked about stars. And, hey, you need crepe myrtle and azaleas! You must have live oaks with branches hanging to the ground. And the dumpsters, filled with the remains of croissants and crawfish, po-boys and muffulettas!*

"Sweetie, I changed my mind about Minnesota," Ruby cooed.

"Who said anything about Minnesota?" George couldn't remember sparrow droppings.

As the September rain intensified, Ruby and George swooped

After the Floods

off in search of thicker foliage and the alligator dragged himself toward the river. Later that night, thunder cracked in the darkness and water rose in the streets, causing people to park their cars on the neutral ground. Kat worked her shift, and the fat man who had covered Kyle's body with a sheet had difficulty sleeping and stared at his ceiling.

Birdie and The Phoenix

Hard Times in April

Let me introduce myself. I'm Lars Johnson. You can't see me, since it's just my voice on paper, and that might be a good thing. My nose lies over to one side, and the left eye is higher than the other. I have a face by Picasso, except that Picasso's name was Vietnam. Some of you remember we had a war there. But it's too bad my voice is just ink marks. My speech used to be pretty good. It goes up and down a little, the way we do in Minnesota, but my wife always said it was deep and expressive, God rest her soul.

I used to be Mayor of Cold Beak, and there were various town meetings where I'd stand in front of an audience and say a few words. The start was always shaky, and then things would smooth out and the deep and expressive part began. I'm older now, shaking a little even when there's no audience. So that's something to go on if you want to build a picture of me in your mind.

Oh, and put some hair on top of that Picasso. I still have my hair, and it takes me to Gopher's Barber Shop, where most of the fact, blather, and speculation that go into this story were first stirred together like batter.

· · ·

After the Floods

I'm going to tell you about the summer when Birdella May took on the April flood, saved Cold Beak, and sent Father Time spinning out of whack. I was already finished being a mayor then, so I had nothing better to do than try to write about my town. The flood was the New Hope River rising over its banks for a look-see, and it got as high as the railings on the county-road bridge, the Barton Memorial Bridge, before it decided it had seen enough. Decades ago, Robert Barton donated a chunk of land to Cold Beak and got the bridge named after him in return. He was the grandfather to Birdie and her brother, Homer, who lived together because neither had married.

In the low parts of town there were canoes in the streets and muddy water crawling five feet up the sides of buildings. A lot of homes were damaged, and cars too, and a few businesses closed their doors and floated away for good. I suppose four or five feet of water and no flood insurance can sort of spoil one's outlook.

Birdie helped as best she could at the church, which God had built on a hill just in case. People were given places to sleep in the church, or they could pick up food and blankets, and day-care kids scrambled about amidst a clutter of board games, rubber balls, and building blocks. I say 'as best she could' because Birdie was a large woman with mobility issues. She couldn't climb into the cab of Homer's pickup, so he rigged a motor to an old leather chair that hoisted her on rails into the cargo area. Once she was in place, Homer would mess with her by making a display of checking the tires. She'd respond by shooting her mock frown down from under blond curls that popped out like springs from old furniture.

At first, folks helped each other a lot after the flood, except for the Sowers. They swarmed together like gnats on their eighty acres outside of town and didn't give a rip about the rest of us.

Birdie and The Phoenix

There were rumors of strange happenings out there, and some folks speculated that Sowers might even have caused the flood by making You-Know-Who angry. I disputed that. God must have learned how to aim a flood by now, what with all the practice. Anyway, pretty soon the energy of people in town just leaked away, almost like how the flood itself had leaked away, and then, as crows watched from branches and power lines, a malaise settled on the town like ashes.

Things that could have happened, hauling away debris or cleaning walls and floors, these things languished undone, and people moped on their porches or in front of their TV sets. Old Willy Berg, who lived with his daughter, Hulda, took to his bed and stopped eating. By the time Birdie heard about it and went to visit him, Willy looked like crumpled paper. Hulda had a boy to take care of, so Birdie got Dr. Shintz to visit Willy and kick him out of bed. But Willy was just one example of the general lethargy.

So even though the sun was shinning, it was a ghostly town that Pete came to a month later, his old Ford pickup loaded with even older household items, a fridge, a gas stove, a sofa, and a bed. He bumped and rattled over the Barton Memorial and past the water tower, then dodged a few of Main Street's many fine potholes, some of which had been in place for years and even had names, like craters on the moon. All along Main, Pete was welcomed by dried mud that still caked the bottom of store fronts, many of them displaying "CLOSED" signs in dusty windows.

• • •

Pete slid the pickup into a diagonal space in front of Gopher's Barber Shop. His first social event in Cold Beak, which occurred as he climbed out of the cab, was to knock a bag from Mattie's arms as she loaded her groceries into her car. There

After the Floods

was no glass to break, but a head of lettuce saw its chance to bound off under the car and settle in a puddle in one of the lesser, unnamed cavities.

"Damn," Pete said. "I'm sorry. Let me help."

Mattie, a spiffy woman in her early thirties, had moved to town to be independent after a belly-up marriage in Minneapolis. You didn't offer to help Mattie. You stood clear and kept your mouth shut. Once, when it was Mattie's turn to be discussed, one of the boys in the barber shop suggested that signs should be posted at the edge of town to warn strangers about her.

"I'll handle it," she replied gruffly, wrestling with her bags, stooping for the lettuce, dropping her keys, shaking water off the lettuce, and in general giving Pete a demonstration in just how clumsy a doofus he had been.

"Well, I'm sorry," he said.

"Don't apologize. My ex was a warehouse of apologies."

"Sorry."

"You're digging a hole, mister, and I have a fascinating life to live."

With that as a parting pleasantry, Mattie backed onto Main Street and sped off. I doubt if Pete was bothered. I imagine him stepping onto the curb, checking his watch that didn't work, and taking a look around.

Across the street from Gopher's Barber Shop was the office of *The Weekly Peep*, our newspaper, although detractors had other names for it, other sounds a body can make. Next to *The Peep* was Birdie's Bakery, with a closed sign in the window, and nearby were Homer's Hardware and Fred's Feed and Fertilizer. Despite the fancy sound effects in the names, all of the buildings were small, no nonsense buildings of wood or vinyl siding. A

Birdie and The Phoenix

person lacking Pete's rural upbringing might have experienced a sinking of the spirit.

Pete went into Gopher's B.S., as we called it, glanced at the clock on the wall, and asked if it would be a long wait, a reasonable enough question since Homer and Fred sat by the wall, both in jeans and sweatshirts, Fred's shirt an orange billboard for Fred's Feeds.

"Long wait," was the reply, but that was from Gopher's parrot, who made frequent assertions from a cage by the window.

"Nah," Gopher said, "don't listen to that bird. The boys here just come in to chat like there's nothing better to do. I run the town rumor mill here."

"This is Gopher's answer to Fox News," Homer volunteered, and it is true that the barber shop was a theater in which fact and fable continually staged their high-school play.

Pete sat in the pruning chair, and Gopher flourished the barber's bib, tucked it snug around Pete's neck, and flipped on the electric clipper.

"I'd like you to do it with the scissors," Pete said, "so's it'll be long on the sides. Don't want white walls."

"In Cold Beak we buzz it right down to the skin, so it'll last," Gopher said, stepping back to get a fuller look at this strange stranger. "Show him that nice, modern haircut, Fred."

Fred tugged off his feed cap, displaying bristles and a grin. No doubt he confirmed Pete's commitment to the scissors. Once Gopher began experimenting with the unfamiliar tool, Pete said that he had come to town to meet up with his older brother, Ole Swenson, and inquired about directions to his house.

"Well," Gopher began, "when a stranger comes to town and don't even want a Cold Beak haircut . . ."

After the Floods

"What sort of guy don't know his own brother's address?" Fred wanted to know.

Of course they were just messing with him, and Homer rummaged in his jeans and produced a cell phone.

"Ole? Homer down at the B.S. Guy here says he's your brother. Won't let Gopher give him a real haircut . . . Yeah, kinda funny looking . . . Okay, talk to ya."

So it was established that Pete was really Ole Swenson's brother, directions out to Ole's house were conveyed, and Pete went on his way once Gopher had snipped around with the scissors for a few minutes.

"Must be odd, moving to a town that's half shut down," Homer said, reaching in his pocket for a pack of gum.

"When is you sister going to get her bakery fired up again?" Gopher asked.

"She's gonna let Marge Swanson manage it. Birdie's got bigger plans," Homer replied. "She's evolving."

Fred and Homer talked for a time about getting back to work, and then, as the sun inched itself around to the west, the parrot dozed in his cage, and Gopher swept the floor, the conversation drifted to fishing.

Ole's Big Plan

William Ferguson was the editor of *The Weekly Peep*, and I imagine him turning away from his paper shredder—he was forever shredding papers like a man with dark secrets—to see Pete leave the B.S., climb into his pickup, and lumber down Pothole Way, as Main Street had come to be called. Ferguson kept an eye on things, as did most of the crows that lined the edge of his roof

Birdie and The Phoenix

like surveillance cameras. Two at the far end of the building were involved only with each other, and you almost thought they were talking.

Folks often wondered how bits of their private lives had become embalmed in *The Peep*. An argument between friends, a distant cousin's health problems, a social blunder at a party, any such animal, dead and dissected, might gaze back at you with glazed eyes from the newspaper at the end of the week, sort of like taxidermy on a wall.

When Ferguson wasn't peering through the lettering on his window or shredding mysterious documents, he read big-city newspapers, not out of a thirst for knowledge but instead out of a melancholy dissatisfaction with his life in a town where all the men wear old jeans and talk mainly about fish they've caught. To hear Ferguson, you'd think we had manure coming out our ears. Maybe his yearning for the big city was only a decorative sort of yearning, one of those characteristics, like a mysterious past, that people fabricate and wear in order to be less ordinary. In any case, it was flaunted like a reproach to the rest of us, so much so that Ferguson gave self-esteem a bad name.

"In New York they have museums . . . with paintings," he might mutter to himself, or to Seth Hogan, his young assistant.

"Yes," Seth might respond, "but we have Gopher's!"

"God, I live where we have Gopher's."

Ferguson often looked at you like you were a smudge, and Seth's attempts at good humor were water off Ferguson's styling gel, which he applied liberally. His hair was Liberace meets Donald Trump, and on his desk, where another person might have kept a photo of a loved one, Ferguson kept a framed mirror. A drawer contained cologne from Paris.

I imagine his face being sucked into the mirror by supernatu-

After the Floods

ral forces, elongating as it goes like something drifting toward a black hole. A mockingbird will attack its own reflection in a window, but mocking people usually go the other way, loving their reflections like that guy by the water in mythology. Ferguson was his descendant.

• • •

So Ferguson and his crows watched Pete head down Main Street that day. Pete's brother, Ole, lived in a small house on the east side of town surrounded by a yard full of birds. During the winter, owls had migrated down from Canada in search of rodents, but then the spring flood seemed to turn our town into a magnet for all kinds of birds. Even mockingbirds had made their way up from Dixie to join the party. Cold Beak had become an unofficial refuge for everything that flapped or chirped, and when Pete chugged to a stop at the house, a score of robins lifted off from Ole's front yard to join an even larger choir in the maple tree.

Pete stood for a moment examining the neighborhood and listening to the kids play Marco Polo. We have some small people in town, people born with genetic issues, and perhaps Pete noticed one of them in a yard. Then Ole exploded from his front door, running as fast as a man of forty-two who likes his burgers and fries is likely to run.

"Am I glad to see you!" Ole shouted as Pete examined the insect-splattered window and grill of his pickup.

"Lot of bugs between there and here," Pete said.

Ole eyed the old truck. "Still?" he asked, panting from his brief sprint. "Looks to me like you got most of them."

"Nah. There's plenty left."

"Forget the bugs," Ole said, delivering a brotherly punch to

32

Birdie and The Phoenix

the arm. "I signed the deal yesterday! Couldn't wait on you dragging your tail along the county roads." He pulled Pete by the arm toward a car parked in the driveway. "Climb in, I'll show ya."

Pete shoved a few candy wrappers and a Coke can onto the floor, as Ole explained that Pete could buy half of his restaurant for a dollar.

"We'll be co-owners like we planned!" Ole affirmed, his round face glowing with optimism like a headlight.

What had been a plan in Ole's mind had been to Pete merely the blowing of a little smoke into the phone, and it was probably hard for him to wrap his thoughts around being a restaurant owner that afternoon as Ole drove him through the dried mud that was Cold Beak. As the car paused at an intersection, Pete contemplated an old Chevy abandoned on the sidewalk. It was splattered up to the windows with mud and spackled on top by an industrious crew of birds. An emaciated collie poked around by a porch.

"If I owned half that dog," Pete declared, "I'd feed my half."

"Yeah," Ole replied, "it's a shame. A few businesses are gone, and some people have moved away. But hey, that's why we're getting such a good deal!"

Pete watched his brother mop his forehead with a red bandana. Ole had come out of the womb with a red bandana and a sweating face. Or else he stole that bandana pretty quick afterwards.

"It's been hard on the Iron Range, too," Pete said. "The ground is running out of ore. There are folks up there been eating crow soup, and that ain't just an expression."

If Pete had been talking to a stranger, he could have said more about life on the Iron Range. The brothers' father had died of mesothelioma, a cancer caused by asbestos in the ore, and recently state health officials had concealed the resurgent number

33

After the Floods

of victims of this disease in the mining community. Ore meant more disease, and less ore meant poverty.

As the car swung into the parking lot, Pete's spirits, already riding low in the water, sunk a bit more. Ole's "good deal" was a deserted and dilapidated Kentucky Fried Chicken place out on the northwest edge of town. An old wooden stork lay on its side by the door.

"That thing arrive in the flood?" Pete asked, gesturing at the stork.

"Nah," Ole said. "But whatchya think of the building?"

"Oh man . . . I don't know if I'm up for it."

They walked around and through the building, Ole pointing this way and nodding that way as he shared his newly acquired insights into architecture and decoration.

"I figure we put mirrors over those windows, or maybe some of those red felt pictures. We could put a painting on the ceiling like that church in Italy. It'll be a supper club with candles and everything. I know a guy in the Cities who will sell me a suit of armor to put by the door and give the place a romantic atmosphere. Whadya think?"

"Do you," Pete asked, "know the first minnow-in-a-pond about running a restaurant?"

"This here is a business opportunity wagging its tail and yapping at you to take it home. I'm going to make this work come hell or high water, and *that* ain't just an expression around here. Besides, we got Mattie on the team. We can build a supper club, or sit on our butts and mope."

Pete probably weighed the options and found moping to be the more attractive, but before he could respond, Homer's pickup clattered into the parking lot with Birdie perched on her cushioned throne in back. Oscar, of course, was on a bench beside her. Oscar, who had recently returned from Iraq with a bad leg, had known Birdie for years, and folks kept finding chances for him to shed light on whether he was courting her. But Oscar didn't shed light. He was the kind that gives off mostly fog.

"See you got that stork you were talking about!" Homer exclaimed, heaving himself from the cab. Homer was a big man, and once Ferguson was heard to say that he was strong as an ox and twice as smart.

"Owner of the miniature golf place by Hibbing sold it cheap," Ole explained. "Good as new, except for where kids splashed paint on her butt."

"She'll look real good when you get her cleaned," Homer said. "You gonna call this place The Stork Club then?" Homer flopped his elephant trunk of an arm over the door as he talked.

Ole said that he didn't want his club to be confused with a place in Paris, and that he'd probably call it The Phoenix in memory of his trip to Arizona. Then introductions were made. Homer and Pete said they'd met already, which Ole knew but had forgotten in all the excitement. Homer kidded about Pete not wanting a real haircut. Birdie pulled a tin of snoose from her jacket and offered it to Pete, who explained that he'd quit.

"I don't have all afternoon to be the main attraction on a Mardi Gras float," Birdie said, "so I say we cut to the chase." She liked to talk like big-city folks.

"What chase would that be?" Ole asked.

"I've been hearing about your restaurant plans, and I want to offer my services, my secret theatrical skills." Birdie left the secret hanging like a cobweb, focusing those moon eyes down from her throne under that bed-spring hair.

After the Floods

"My sister wants to be a stripper to lose weight," Homer explained. "I told her that strippers have to dance, that it ain't just a matter of climbing out of those bib overalls, but she's determined."

Then Birdie explained how the boys had an opportunity to be part of history because it wouldn't be the sort of strip club that exploits poor girls who can't find a decent job. This would be a club that would help big people have pride while they trimmed themselves down.

The guys were quiet when she finished, and she sat there on her throne giving them the doe-eye. Ole adjusted his feed cap and stared off at the clouds over the Mobile station, and Pete expected him to say how a cloud looked like this animal or that. The power lines served as bleachers for the crows that gathered to watch and heckle. Finally, Birdie went on to explain how she pictured it all.

"The way I picture it all, we divide the club in two. Folks don't want to eat their meat and potatoes with a big old fat girl yanking her clothes off and shaking her stuff right there."

Birdie paused, maybe to picture herself shaking her stuff, and then her laughter broke like surf on the shore of a late afternoon.

"They don't want their kids asking questions," she concluded. "So the strip club is a separate room."

Ole was back to dabbing his face with the bandana, and you could have heard a moth fart. Finally Ole said how he didn't make business decisions right off the bat, and how he'd have to think on whether the town was ready for so much innovation.

"Might as well surrender right now, boys" Homer said, climbing back into the truck. "Arguing with Birdie is like arguing with boulders."

He turned out to be right about that. Homer is a whole lot

Birdie and The Phoenix

smarter than an ox. The pickup careened out of the parking lot, causing Birdie to grab the arms of her throne and causing Oscar to grab Birdie.

In the distance the orange and purple rags of a sunset draped themselves over a hill. It would be a stretch to call anything in Minnesota a mountain, but the land does shrug its shoulders here and there. The shrug out west of town is called Bestrom's Hill, and my friends and I used to hike there when we were kids, stopping to admire horses in a field where an abandoned barn sank back into the grass like an ancient frigate in a book. I remember how the sun would let its golden hair down into those fields, making me think of that girl in the tower.

Anyway, that's the direction the pickup was headed when it flung Oscar and Birdie around on its way out of the parking lot.

Bad Press

Only God and CNN know how Ferguson got wind of Birdie's plan so fast, but in a couple of days the headline in *The Peep* read "Not In Our Town." Maybe he really did have those crows trained to snoop. The talk at the barber shop was all about how Birdie would react to Ferguson's broadside, but Homer assured everyone that Birdie wouldn't be deterred by a pipsqueak with glue in his hair.

Birdie herself got Oscar to drive her to Betty's Fabrics to shop for material for her stage costume. The costume had to be red, white, and blue to signal her proper intentions. How a floor show in a restaurant relates to patriotism was not clearly stated, and folks were too polite to ask. In a small town, people can't challenge one another at every turn and then just disappear into the crowd.

After the Floods

"Does this bring out my natural radiance?" she asked, holding a fabric sample beneath her chin and cocking her head.

Before Betty could respond, Ann and Rachel appeared by Birdie's side. Ann was eight and Rachel five. They had a single mom and were threadbare. Their grandmother had taken them out for air that day, and she had become intrigued with a display of buttons. The girls clutched candy bars in grimy hands and gazed up at Birdie out of faces smeared mainly with chocolate.

"Grandma says you're going to take your clothes off in a restaurant," Ann declared. "She says you belong in your bakery."

"My-my, the town does miss its calories," Birdie replied. "Have you been eavesdropping?"

"No, she said it to my face. She said I shouldn't talk to you."

"But here you are! How lucky I am!"

"Billy Grindahl had me take my clothes off behind the garage," Ann offered.

Before Birdie could respond to that news flash, the children were tugged away by their grandmother, little Rachel turning to display an alarmingly large, candy-coated tongue.

"Children can be mean," Betty said, "but they don't know any better, and sometimes they're so cute."

"Yes," Birdie replied, "it's natures way of seeing to it we don't kill them." Of course she didn't really mean it.

• • •

Pete found himself in the fray when he and Ole went to The Brown Ungulate to meet with Mattie. The Ungulate was a steak and ale place on the edge of town, and it had a life-sized synthetic cow above the door, one of those inspiring artifacts of rural America. Mattie and Hulda were waitresses. As the brothers entered, Hulda handed a tray down to a small woman, Barbara

Birdie and The Phoenix

Fox, also a waitress. When Barbara slides a tray onto a table, it's almost at her eye level, but she does a good job. She's been my waitress more than once.

Pete, of course, had no way of knowing that he was about to meet the person whose lettuce he'd sent spinning into a pothole full of mud. Although Mattie shot him a look when he tried to help her with her chair, their new partnership got off to a fairly smooth start. Mattie had worked in the restaurant of a Radisson Hotel in Minneapolis, and she would oversee the kitchen at The Phoenix.

"All the disputants are here today," Mattie remarked once she had adjusted her chair. "Malvolio is over by the window." She nodded in the direction of our newspaper man, who sat alone in his buttoned-down shirt, silk tie, and televangelist's hair that got chauffeured down to Minneapolis twice a month for maintenance, no Gopheresque haircut for him.

"I thought his name was Ferguson," Pete said, causing Mattie to roll her eyes.

"You never read Tom Clancy?" she asked.

They talked about whether Birdie's kind offer should be accepted, rejected, or tabled for further discussion, and about the PR issues Ferguson had created. Pete said that on the one hand he wasn't enthusiastic for controversy but on the other hand didn't want a rooster gooped with pomade telling him what to do. Mattie responded that it was a good thing Pete didn't have a third hand or his decisions would get complicated.

Eventually, Ferguson sauntered by their table to espouse family values and to forecast the embarrassment to the town if a large woman who belongs in her bakery were to embark on an entertainment career at the age of thirty-five. Mattie explained that Birdie was a grown woman and would exercise good judg-

After the Floods

ment. Ferguson countered that she was an *over*grown woman, whereupon Mattie likened him to beetle dung. Ole jumped in by asking Ferguson if he could see his own reflection in the sacramental wine. The following day, opinions at the B.S. were divided about the sharpness of that dart, Fred wondering what wine had to do with anything.

In any case, Ferguson pranced away, and Mattie explained to Ole and Pete that Birdie simply wanted to be somebody, wanted to be noticed and respected. To Mattie, it had become a women's rights issue, and the guys agreed that Birdie would be invited to start working on her dance moves.

• • •

Later that afternoon, the reunited brothers sat on Ole's porch with Ole's St. Bernard, Swede, curled up beneath the American flag that dangled from a pole above the mailbox. The words "Marco" and "Polo" echoed through the neighborhood, as children crouched behind trees and raced like rabbits across lawns. Pete wasn't thrilled to have landed in a village fraught with controversy, and he suggested that the brothers take the next day off from the project of sending Cold Beak straight to hell.

"Let's go fishing instead," Pete suggested, staring off into Carl Ellison's front yard with its array of carved-wood statues.

"Everything okay?" Ole asked, apparently tabling the fishing question.

"Thinking about Irene is all."

"She was a good one."

"Marco," a small voice called from behind a cedar tree.

"The best thing that ever happened in my life," Pete affirmed.

It doesn't require a lot of words to add up to a conversation

Birdie and The Phoenix

in Cold Beak, and the brothers fell silent. What more was there to say? Pete's wife, Irene, had died a year ago, and he had lost his job in mining a few months later. Now he had finally moved away from the Iron Range. Ole scratched the dozing Swede behind an ear, and a mockingbird took flight from the maple tree, flashing the white patches on its wings and its fanning tail.

"You're a good old pal," Ole said, "best dog around, aren't you?"

Across the street a row of cedars moved in the breeze like green flames, and the Marco Polo game echoed here and there. Ole pulled out his cell phone and punched in a number.

"Mattie? It's Ole here. We're going fishing tomorrow. You off work? . . . Nah, nothing too early . . . On the river . . . Great, pick you up around nine."

Ole flipped the phone closed, and Pete stared at him as though he had just turned into a lizard or a Republican.

"We're a team now," Ole declared by way of justification. "It'll be fine. Just don't offer to help her with her fishing gear."

"I get the idea," Pete replied, reaching over to give Swede a pat.

Two children came skipping and stumbling around the side of the house, the Marco Polo game over.

"The Sowers are crazy people and they should be chased away," the boy said. He was Randy Colson, a nine-year-old rapidly absorbing the opinions of a sour mother.

"My dad says they have rights too," Sally Angstrom replied.

"Do not."

"Do too."

Sally paused and stooped to pick a dandelion, wishing on it, perhaps, as she blew its smoky spores into the air. Then the two of them skipped and danced down the sidewalk, continuing the exchange on human rights.

After the Floods

It's a world of wishes, Pete thought. The brothers went inside, and soon a wind from the west pulled a patchwork quilt of clouds over the town. The twilight was sleepy with rain, but that was okay because most of Cold Beak goes to bed early anyway.

They All Go Fishing

Pete was awake early the next day, as darkness lifted like an eyelash. He tiptoed around the kitchen, and finally decided to let Swede be his tour guide around the neighborhood. The clouds had tumbled on through, and the morning had brightened by the time Pete and Swede returned to the house. Eventually the foursome (since you have to count Swede) found themselves at the New Hope River, the humans wading in hip boots or sitting on the bank.

Swede pursued his usual pastime of napping, as ducks wobbled to and fro on the shore and paddled about in the water and as mourning doves exchanged calls in the trees. Sometimes, as sunlight trembled on the water, dragonflies hovered by the fishing lines then darted away, delicately blue and mysterious.

On the far bank, a man and three women sat with poles in the water. They were too far away for careful scrutiny, but to Pete they seemed out of place. There was something abject (even for Cold Beak) in the demeanor of the women, and perhaps in the way they were dressed.

"Anyone you guys know?" Pete asked, gesturing with his pole.

"Sowers," Ole replied.

"Assholes," Mattie said by way of clarification. "And I say that with no disrespect."

Birdie and The Phoenix

"They're a group of nutjobs who own a few acres beyond that hill," Ole explained, nodding vaguely over the water. "I think they see angels in the woods—stuff like that."

"Probably meth heads?" Pete asked.

"Don't know," Mattie replied.

"Should find out," Ole added.

Then Pete got a strike that turned out to be a stick swirling in the current. They spent the morning catching sticks, while back in town Ferguson went on his own fishing expedition. First he climbed the hill to call on Rev. Olson in her office at the Lutheran Church, reminding her of her moral duties as the town's spiritual leader. Sally pointed out that he might try writing some positive commentary in *The Weekly Peep*, such as the fact that Homer's Hardware and Fred's Feeds were both giving interest-free credit to victims of the flood. Ferguson scoffed and told her that two of the church's wealthiest contributors had signed a petition to condemn the Birdie show.

Next he stopped by Sheriff Mike Maki's office. Mike's dad had been sheriff when I was mayor.

"I ain't gonna lecture Birdella May Borguson!" Mike shouted. "Are you out of your mind? Lighten up, Bill. Here, have a Nut Goodie. It's better than Paxil." Maki rummaged in a drawer and tossed him a candy bar.

"*The Weekly Peep* . . ."

"Don't gimme your *Weekly Peep*! You move to town smelling like bubble gum, you tack up your master's degree in pontification, and all we get from you is criticism. When I run out of critics, I'll have another daughter!" It was just the kind of thing his dad would have said.

Ferguson left Maki's office. With two strikes against him, his

43

After the Floods

dobber was a little down. His third stop was the home of Mayor Carl Best, whom he found in the backyard landscaping the area around a small goldfish pond. Best was noncommittal, but agreed to take up the issue of Birdie's proposed "floor show," as it was now being called, with the Chamber of Commerce.

Ferguson returned to his office convinced that reasoning with the town's leadership was like discussing stock options with a gaggle of geese. His grip on that wiggly creature called public opinion was slipping, and I picture him sweating puddles before the mirror on his desk.

• • •

Meanwhile, on the opposing front, Birdie, June, and Betty, who referred to themselves as The Large Ladies Club, picked out sports bras at Barbara's Big Girls Shop and headed for 12 Hour Fitness for their first workout. They stood in the doorway of the workout room in their colorful new exercise outfits and contemplated the young and the buff pumping iron, grunting, and shouting observations such as, "It's all you, man!" Slowly the noises subsided as eyes swiveled toward the new kids on the block.

"Don't stop what you're doing," Birdie said. "We ain't here to distract you with our charms."

"I like that one over there," June remarked, gesturing with her head.

"How about the one on the bar?" Birdie said, looking at a man in gravity boots who hung by his feet while talking on a cell phone. "I like my men upside down."

As the ladies walked through the room, they pinched biceps and selected favorites as though shopping for vegetables. Betty paused by a slim girl doing crunches on an incline board.

44

Birdie and The Phoenix

"Sweetheart," Betty said, "if we could just match my boobs with your abs!"

"I'm saving for new boobs," the girl confided.

"Well, if you ever need a donor, dearie, be sure to let me know."

Birdie circled an unusually buff fellow in a sleeveless, skin-tight and provocatively black workout shirt. His biceps were intricately inked soccer balls.

"I never! Those buttocks!" she exclaimed as her roaming eyes crashed to a stop beneath his belt. "Have you ever been in show business?"

"Ah . . . not in public," the young man replied.

Birdie touched him lightly and informed him that her people would contact him. Then the three ladies made their way to the stationary bikes at the far end of the room, where they peddled for a few minutes with much stopping, starting, and puffing.

"That can't be the same woman who worked in the bakery," the guy with the tattooed biceps remarked.

"She used to just smile and give you a cookie," the slim girl of modest boobs replied.

In a few minutes, there was commotion in the women's locker room as the Large Ladies struggled to remove their soggy sports bras. Birdie wondered if there was a chain saw handy, and June declared that she was about to pee her pants. The rest was laughter, confirming that girls do just want to have fun.

• • •

Later that afternoon, two teenaged boys taking a short cut through the vacant lot beside Birdie's home paused to look over her fence.

"What the *heck* is that?" one boy asked.

"Damn! What *is* that?" the other exclaimed.

"I ain't never!" the first boy muttered.

45

After the Floods

Birdie's sports bra billowed like a sail on the clothes line.
"Sort of like a halter?" a boy asked.
"Nah, couldn't be."
"Then what the heck . . ."

• • •

Overnight, Cold Beak had become a theatre of political warfare, and there were even yard signs, both camps using red, white, and blue and therefore accusing one another of stealing intellectual property. The following day, the Large Ladies, who rivaled Ferguson in their ability to manage opinion, made their own promotional stops.

At the Lutheran Church, the gals allowed Rev. Olson to pray with them for guidance, and judging from the hugs and kisses on the church steps as they departed, God had okayed the floor show. Next, the ladies approached the long arm of the law via the stomach, clamoring into Maki's office with pastries, pies, and smiles as wide as summer. When they left, Birdie pulled out her tin of snoose to celebrate.

The decisive victory occurred a few days later, when Birdie made her official presentation to the Chamber of Commerce. First, she explained that her intention had never been to take *everything* off. Then, aided by pie charts and graphs projected on a screen by the ever-present Oscar, she delivered an inspiring oration on the role that a supper club with a floor show could play in the economic renewal of Cold Beak. It would be morning in Cold Beak, she proclaimed, the dawning of a bright new era!

Cheers and exclamations followed her summation, and many a Cold Beak eye was moist. Mayor Best, hearing the applause and sensing the drift of things like a well oiled weathervane, overcame his confusions and aligned himself with the future.

Birdie and The Phoenix

Of course there were times when I was mayor that I ignored the weather entirely, and that's not good either.

Anyway, this was the moment when a new sort of flood filled Cold Beak, a flood of enthusiasm and energy that replaced the malaise that Pete had driven his old pickup into on that first day. Ferguson crept away from the Chamber meeting unnoticed, his invisible dobber dragging behind him. He was heard to mutter something about Birdie "playing politics," the political combatant's retort of last resort.

"What you think, Lars?" Mayor Best asked me on the steps of City Hall after the meeting.

"I can't find the words to describe your leadership," I replied.

Times Goes Nuts

The truth is, the villain in the story wasn't really Ferguson, it was just the circumstances themselves, the bad economy, the stale attitudes, and that bit of jealousy that stays rooted in all of us. Even after the Chamber embraced Birdie's floor show, there were a few grumblers, and a few of the oppositional yard signs remained stubbornly stuck in front lawns, reminders of the staying-power of self righteousness.

Elvira Emerson said some pretty rude things in the beauty shop. She was a small person, but the problem others had with her had nothing to do with her genetic misfortune. Elvira was someone who never had a thought blow through her wig without it coming out her mouth. She worked hard at being annoying, but never smiled, no matter how successful she'd been. Elvira had a husband, also small, but no one knew why he'd fallen in with her, there being others to pick from. He never drank much.

After the Floods

One time the topic in the B.S. was to imagine a situation where you wouldn't mind being alone with her. Ole came up with being stuck on the moon with the campfire dying and the other food gone, but Homer said that Elvira's company would not be worth the nutritional benefit. Fred argued, missing the point as he often does, that you can't build a fire on the moon.

The reality is that Elvira's opinions made little difference, and after Birdie's success with the Chamber of Commerce, Ferguson merely went back to his office to brood, to gaze in his mirror, and to dream about living in a big city amidst the glamour and glitter that a man with French cologne deserved. On the Birdie issue, he was smart enough to quit while he was behind.

• • •

This is the point in the story where time started to slip out of whack in Cold Beak. People didn't realize it all at once, but the more observant citizens marveled at how quickly the renovation of the old KFC occurred. For three days, as assorted birds watched from roof tops and branches, sawdust and plaster filled the air and delivery trucks raced in and out of the parking lot. Oscar planted saplings around the lot one afternoon, and the following morning they had grown two feet and were spreading their arms. For observant folks, it was like watching a film in fast motion, but not fast enough to seem like a complete violation of the laws of nature. And yet people marveled.

"Hmmm," Byron Olson mused from his nearby gas station at the end of the first day.

"Well, glory be!" Edith Vines exclaimed as she passed by in her Ford Escort on the second day.

"If that don't beat all get-out!" Marvin Updahl avowed from the cab of his truck on day three.

Birdie and The Phoenix

On the fourth day, with work nearly finished, Pete pulled into the parking lot, stepped out of his pickup, and admired the refurbished building with its spanking new addition to house the lounge and the floor show. The stork had a new perkiness about it as well, having been scrubbed and mounted above the door as if in challenge to the cow at The Brown Ungulate. Beside the entrance to the parking lot, a large neon sign announced The Phoenix Supper Club and Lounge in curling script.

Inside the front door, Pete found Lancelot, the suit of armor that Ole had purchased in St. Paul, lying in pieces waiting for all the king's men to put him together. Mattie rummaged about the kitchen, checking off appliances and equipment in a notebook.

"Yo," Pete said, stepping over debris and into the kitchen, "everything in order?"

"Over there you got your freezer and your fridge, and there are your ovens and griddles," she replied. "That box in the middle of the floor is full of pans and ladles. It'll be a little cramped, but this will be the best small-town restaurant on the river."

After pausing to admire her kitchen again, she asked where Ole and Homer were.

"Sitting in a boat somewhere dangling worms in the water. It's SFD, the seasonal fishing disorder."

"It doesn't afflict you?" Mattie asked.

"I thought I'd come here for a scolding."

Mattie eyed him suspiciously. "You better walk carefully, Peter Swenson. Next thing you know, you and I will have a real conversation." I imagine her doing a quick little smile, her teeth flashing like the white top of a wave on the lake. I saw her smile like that once myself.

"I'm not afraid . . . much. Can I put this somewhere for you?" Pete asked, indicating the box of pans.

After the Floods

"Oh, I'll get it later."

Pete lifted the box, struggled with it a moment, and then set it on the counter.

"There," he said, "that'll be more convenient."

"Sure," Mattie said hesitantly, "thanks."

They walked back through the dining room, and Pete stepped through the doorway into the Antler's Lounge, furnished with bar stools, tables and chairs, a juke box, and the heads of deer protruding from plaques on every wall.

"I officially hate those heads and their permanent stare," Mattie said. "Why do men kill things and put them where they'll stare at you?"

"Taxidermy is the highest form of praise?"

They were silent for a moment, and then Pete spoke quietly.

"Me and Irene would go dancing when we were young, but I haven't danced in a while. She died, you know."

"I heard," Mattie said, "sorry. What time you got?"

Pete shrugged without looking at his watch. "This watch doesn't work," he said.

"I'm the Juke Box Bitch around here," Mattie declared as they turned to leave. "No one puts new music in that juke without my permission."

"Roger that. Country western?"

"Sparingly."

By the outer door, Pete paused over the rubble that was sometimes Lancelot. "What's with Lancelot?" he asked.

"Oscar had him standing pretty good yesterday. Maybe a mouse burped in the night."

"He needs propping up," Pete said. "I'll build him a skeleton."

"Don't bother. Lancelot is Oscar's toy."

Birdie and The Phoenix

Birdie Prepares and Mattie Mopes

What sort of music would Mattie impose upon the lonely drinkers in the Antler's Lounge? More interestingly, why did Pete decide to poke around The Phoenix when the other men had gone fishing? Why did Mattie fail to complain when he had the audacity to help her with the box of pans, only to reject his offer to put Humpty Lancelot together again? Was he happy to be batting 500, or did he feel that his luck had taken a dive into the tank?

A small town must have its rumors, and the freshest one, still in its whisperhood, was that Pete and Mattie were sizing each other up. In due time we will know more about who does and doesn't canoodle, but in the meantime Birdie continued to prepare for her opening night.

Birdie and her brother, Homer, shared a house, like I said, and as Homer sat in the front room reading *Field & Stream,* the sound on the TV muted, the Large Ladies worked on Birdie's costume, their laughter coming to him through a partially open door. Birdie declared that they would need safety pins as big as horse shoes, and Betty replied that she'd been making tents all her life.

"I look like a piñata!" Birdie exclaimed at one point.

Eventually June pulled a CD from her purse, and Homer found himself tapping a foot to "The Stripper." A blouse flew through the open doorway, and then Birdie slid by doing the Funky Chicken. Suddenly, as suddenly as was possible for him, Homer grabbed the remote and turned up the sound.

"Girls!" he called. "They're showing our ad!"

The ladies rushed in to observe two local "actors" (with day jobs at 12 Hour Fitness) in front of a painted backdrop depicting palm trees and a beach. The male invited the female to a

After the Floods

week on the Riviera, only to hear that the Riviera was passé. Next he mentioned the hotel he owned in Tahiti. Still no luck. He then offered a weekend in Cold Beak and dinner at The Phoenix, at which the female turned into a mass of clinging gelatin and stated that all of her many charms were now his. Then an announcer's voice, in an accelerated monotone, provided a phone number for reservations.

Our friends in the living room were jubilant, and Birdie passed her snuff around. Homer probably reached for his gum.

We could turn our attention back to Ferguson, or to Gopher's Barber Shop. And it might be interesting to keep up with Sheriff Maki's doings. But stories, even true ones, have to be selective, and it might be best to keep tabs on Pete and Mattie, who, after leaving Lancelot beside himself on the floor by the front door of the restaurant, had agreed to spend an hour of the following day in the park beside the river.

• • •

The spot they found was near a multi-colored village of structures for children to slide, climb, and squeal on. A few picnic tables and cooking sites completed the scene. Hulda was there with Jeffery, who shouted to Mattie from atop the slide that his dad, serving in the United States Marines, would be home soon. Then Pete and Mattie settled themselves in the grass, and Pete tossed bread to an assortment of robins, crows, and sparrows who had abandoned their sectarian distrust of one another in favor of easy eats. Two snowy egrets, who had apparently followed the mockingbirds north, watched from a nearby cottonwood tree, shocked at the forwardness of the other birds.

"You're a quiet one, mister," Mattie observed.

"I was thinking about this guy I knew who would toss bread

Birdie and The Phoenix

in the air and get gulls to hover around him. It was the year I went to college in Duluth. That's where I met Irene."

"I met my ex in college, too," Mattie said. "I went to Hamline in St. Paul."

"You got kids?"

"No, my ex sowed seeds in other gardens."

"Sorry."

As they talked, mourning doves did their call and response and children played Marco Polo.

"Both species are up to a similar project," Mattie observed. "The difference is that the doves use five syllables and the kids two."

"Me and Irene wanted to have a kid, but then she got cancer in the ovaries. Our house was by a river, but the mining company built a dam and it dried up. Only the wind flows there now. After she died it was like our house was haunted, only it was probably me doing the haunting. It's strange to live with someone who isn't really there anymore."

"So you tossed some stuff in your pickup and came looking for a new life."

Pete thought about that for a moment, and then merely replied that he hadn't seen his brother in a while. They were quiet again.

"I think that memories are like pieces of a song," Pete said. After a pause, he admitted that he didn't quite know what he had meant. I've found that it's like that when I try to express feelings, too. It's like trying to describe a cloud.

Then Mattie stood and offered to show him the site where Carl Best planned to build a boat launch and give tours of the river. They stopped under a tree, where Mattie picked up a broken egg shell.

"Oh, look," she said, "a robin's egg. What a shame." She held the shell out to Pete. "It's the prettiest blue in the world, isn't it?"

After the Floods

"That and the sky," Pete replied.

He looked upward, trying to see the nest but seeing only a dangling branch that the wind had snapped. Then they walked along the path by the river, pausing occasionally for the geese who made their way back and forth from the water to the grass. Then Pete said that he hadn't slept well the previous night.

"How come?"

"Irene. I was lying there thinking about her, and how ungrateful it would be . . . You know."

"Oh say it," Mattie insisted. "You won't break my egg."

Of course Pete wanted to say as little as possible, but he was also forthright enough to want to say something.

"It wouldn't be grateful to look for someone else. She was the best thing in my life, and when I think about her she's like a river running in my thoughts and making a happy sound. I wouldn't want anything else."

Mattie didn't respond, and Pete observed that now she had become the quiet one.

"I'm not going to try to rebuild your life," she said. "I don't fix broken lives."

"That's fine," Pete replied. "I didn't come here for a new life . . . It's strange how people disappear."

"Every time they leave the room."

Further up the path, Mike Maki's sister, Siiri, sat in the grass and watched her new friend, the young man who had moved north from Louisiana to live in the woods, toss a baseball with her son, Sandy.

"That's Siiri Elden," Mattie said. "She's a nurse over at the county hospital. Her ex was as big a clinker as mine, so we hang out a little now and then. Her boy, Sandy, is one smart kid."

The river tumbled by, still fresh and clean, although a few

Birdie and The Phoenix

miles to the south a paper mill had begun the process of modernization, which is to say pollution. A boat bobbed gently in a shoal on the other side.

• • •

I pulled for Pete and Mattie that summer. Each had come to Cold Beak looking to find a new life and escape an old one, a bad marriage for Mattie and a lost one for Pete. And Pete had fled a damaged world, too, where mines maim the earth, miners die of cancer, and rivers are turned into dry wind. Sometimes, in dreams, I imagine that the New Hope River has gone silent. The water is there, but it doesn't move. It's a foolish dream, and it probably has something to do with growing old, but maybe also with what we are doing to the planet. I think that our lives are rivers, turning, joining, and rolling on, and also threatened and vulnerable.

A Digression on Birds

That summer Cold Beak was an ornithologist's heaven and a whole bunch better than Disney Land for the rest of us. We had pipers and pelicans, peacocks and cormorants. One morning, a huge kiwi high-stepped out from behind the hedge in my backyard, causing Spike, my cocker spaniel, to tuck his tail, upset his water bowl, and scramble into his doghouse, where he remained for the afternoon, issuing an occasional yap. Kiwis can't fly, and I don't know how they made their way from Down Under to Minnesota. Maybe they hopped an ocean liner.

Bowerbirds arrived with their skills from half way around the world. They build elaborate shrines from feathers, sticks, and stones. We would find their monuments in the park along the

After the Floods

river, and it seemed incredible that such architecture could have been achieved by a mere bird in search of a mate. Of course men like Donald Trump build towers and empires, but still you had to admire the enterprise of the birds and wish them well in their search for feathered bliss.

We had hummingbirds and jays, tanagers, both scarlet and otherwise, and painted buntings, so named because Mother Nature unleashed her pallet on them. The orange of the orioles, whether from Baltimore or Boise, warmed more than a few chilly hearts in Cold Beak. There were birds with red breasts and yellow, meadowlarks and warblers that sang, crows and gulls that screeched. Feeders and birdbaths appeared as if by magic in yards everywhere, much to Fred's delight, since they could be purchased at Fred's Feed and Fertilizer. Business at Dick's Carwash also spiked.

Most of us marveled and admired, although a few complained. Elvira Emerson had been frightened by an ostrich that wandered into her tulips. Unlike Spike, who merely whimpered, she went to Mayor Best demanding action. Of course an ostrich can be pretty fearsome to a small person like Elvira. Ferguson blew a tire when he hit a pothole while dodging a family of ducks crossing Main Street toward Birdie's Bakery. Even though we always have ducks, he wrote an editorial about the "infestation."

So if time went out of whack that summer, and you'll hear more of that soon, the geographical distribution of our feathered companions also experienced a makeover. Reverend Olson claimed that all of this fussing with nature's furniture simply proved that God is a woman after all, causing the congregation to laugh as she so often did.

But let's get back to Birdie and The Phoenix.

Birdie and The Phoenix

Grand Opening

The day after Pete's hour with Mattie in the park, Pete and Ole jogged on the riverside path near where Mattie had found the broken egg shell. Swede labored along beside the brothers, and birds (both the locals and the new tourists) debated in the trees. The warts on the rocks were turtles sunning.

"I'm whipped," Ole said. They had gone about a quarter of a mile.

"Barely started," Pete managed to say.

"So?"

"Can't just quit."

"Can too."

With that, Ole swerved off the trail, staggered, and spread himself on the grass, where he began to make angels in imaginary snow. Swede and Pete settled in beside him, and Ole fished his red bandana from his pocket and dabbed at his dripping face.

"This getting in shape stuff," Ole complained, "I don't know . . . Don't see the benefit of being wore out. What good is an in-shape dead guy?"

Then the brothers rested on their backs and contemplated the clouds that followed the course of the river in their slow drift southward. The sun came and went, warming them in waves.

"You dating Mattie?" Ole asked.

"She's got a low opinion of the male life form," Pete replied.

"You barely met her."

"So?"

"Can't just quit."

Ducks skidded to a stop on the river, and children in the park played Marco Polo.

"Can't get started," Pete replied.

• • •

57

After the Floods

The grand opening of The Phoenix and of the Birdie show was on the 4th of July. People came in carloads all the way from Duluth and all the way over from New Persiflage, and further off too. The motel was jammed full, and Berry Larson let out plots for the campers in a field where he had forgotten to plant his soy beans. The neon sign, with its blue light and swooping cursive, was lovely, and Sheriff Maki sent Ted, his deputy, over to stand below the sign and direct traffic. Ole wore his suit, a blue flannel number he had bought once with the thought of joining the church.

Birdie was nervous, and no one saw the need to make it worse by telling her that the entertainment critic from the *Minneapolis Star Tribune* would be there to review her act. The critic and his trophy blonde arrived like royalty in a white limousine. The blonde was one of the most beautiful of God's creatures, except maybe for horses. Ole, with much bowing and scraping that had been practiced before a mirror, seated them by Lancelot, propped up now with an inner skeleton of sticks but with his head and arms at angles not quite human. Lancelot held an axe.

"Our very best suit of armor, sir," Ole assured the critic, "brought all the way from England. Perfectly safe. Everything is complimentary tonight, sir, everything. If there is anything I can do, anything at all . . ."

Ole backed off, still bowing and smiling, and nearly stumbled into the lap of Rev. Olson, seated with her husband at a nearby table. The dinner was served from shining new carts, and at 7:30 Ole announced that the premiere performance of the floor show would begin in one half hour in the Antler's Lounge.

Birdie had recruited three young men (including the one who had acted in the TV spot) from 12 Hour Fitness. They called themselves The Clydesdales and opened the show with a

Birdie and The Phoenix

surprisingly rousing bit of bumping, grinding, and discarding of shirts. Birdie's role was a combination of dance steps, Mae West imitations, and commentaries on nutrition and weight loss. For her finale, her dress broke away and billowed through the air, leaving her standing in a red, white, and blue costume with a large feather in back.

I nursed a gin tonic at the bar next to Fred. As he gawked at Birdie, a fly checked out his mouth and then settled in an ear. I suppose you can't depend on a mouth staying open indefinitely.

Pete worked the bar that night, dressed in a new plaid shirt ordered special from L.L. Bean. When only a few customers remained, he looked up from rinsing glasses to see Mattie leaning on the new oak surface. The juke was playing "I Didn't Know What Time It Was," and Mattie sang a few lines in a soft voice.

"Warm like the month of May it was,
And I'll say it was grand.
Grand to be alive, to be young,
To be mad, to be . . . ."

There she broke off in confusion, and Pete asked her if she wanted to dance. She joked about facing the music, and they became the last couple on the floor, circling slowly in the dim light.

"When you talked about that memory river running inside you," Mattie said as they danced, "well, I think your river is a good thing. Loyalty is a good thing."

There was a slice of air between them, and Pete danced awkwardly that night. When the song ended, we went outside to where Ole had set up chairs in back of The Phoenix. The Fourth of July celebration by the river was booming along, and Birdie exclaimed that fireworks had become an art form. Oscar said it was like splashing paint on the sky, and Pete remembered the gulls that had hovered about the head of his old friend in Duluth.

After the Floods

Others probably also read something of their own experiences, emotions, and dreams into the bursting and dissolving beauty of the display. Ole stayed on for a while after the display ended and the rest of us had said goodbye. It was one of those times when Ole's loneliness showed through. I don't know how long he sat there as the stars flowed slowly over the trees and across the night.

• • •

The next day, Homer and Fred charged into Gopher's B.S., brushing past Alligator, who was on his way out smelling of lotion from Gopher's colorful collection. Alligator was the young guy who had moved up from Louisiana to be a hermit. At first he'd been taken for a Sower. But Sowers don't come to town for haircuts, and Gopher and Sheriff Maki (and Maki's sister, Siiri) had both gotten to know him well enough to vouch for his sanity.

In any case, Homer and Fred slipped past him and took chairs along the wall, announcing that they were flummoxed. Homer, who had a Minneapolis newspaper in his hand, said he'd be damned, and the parrot in the cage said he would be as well.

"What are you damned about this time?" Gopher asked, and Homer replied that the critic they'd seen at The Phoenix had actually written about Birdie's show.

"Hope she don't take it too hard," Gopher said as he swept up a sprinkling of Alligator's hair.

Homer explained that the critic actually seemed to like the show, even though the big words made it hard to be sure. Fred asked what words those might be, and Homer quoted the assertion that the show "exposed the social construction of fat within the hegemonic ideology of the fitness industry."

"What do ya suppose that means?" Gopher asked, and Fred said that it was just crazy-guy talk.

60

Birdie and The Phoenix

"Maybe," Homer replied, "but it's positive crazy."

Then Fred took to shooing a fly that buzzed around his head, spilling his Coke in the process and causing Homer to duck away. Fred slipped in the spilt Coke, and as he picked himself up Gopher smashed the fly on his head with a magazine—*Sports Illustrated*, I think it was.

• • •

At about the same time across the street, Ferguson lowered his copy of the Minneapolis newspaper and allowed as how *he'd* be damned.

"What's up, boss?" Seth asked.

"They like it! The *Star Tribune* likes it!"

"That pops your bubble, boss. That leaves *The Peep* looking like a doofus in the cabbage patch scratching his . . ."

"I know what it means, bird brain!" Ferguson replied, slowly and carefully tearing the newspaper in long strips and then examining himself in his mirror, looking for crows' feet or perhaps hoping to dive in and give himself some much needed love.

In the following days, a farmer shopping for feed at Fred's was heard to assert that the floor show was "a mimesis of a longed-for integration of obesity into the ideology of late capitalism." His wife reminded him that "we mustn't forget how Birdie deconstructs that ideology by . . ." Down the block, one of the small people shopping for lingerie voiced her belief that "the concept of fat as metaphor is overly derivative of Susan Sontag," whereas her friend countered that she had been reminded of "Michel Foucault's analysis of the sexually repressive power discourses in Western culture."

In the town square, Sheriff Maki sat on a bench chatting with the young man from New Orleans. Behind them Hulda's boy,

After the Floods

Jeffrey, slapped a tetherball to Ann and stated that "Birdie shows how postmodern primitivism undermines the binary oppositions that structure previous aesthetic assumptions."

"Does not," Ann replied, slapping the ball with all her might.

"Does too," Jeffrey countered, whacking it back to her.

"Gimme a break."

Then they went to Dick Moody's drugstore and bought Cokes.

A Rocket to Tomorrow

When Birdie started her book, that Paglia woman from out East came to help with the spelling and stuff, riding into town in a taxi all the way from Minneapolis International. She was nice. A couple of us took her fishing out at Lake Dakota. She wore black leather slacks and high-heeled boots that were definitely not for fishing, or at least the sort of fishing us folks do, but she caught a perch anyway, a seven incher.

But here's where things started to become strange, where time got clearly out of whack.

Birdie and her spiffy assistant were convinced that they had worked on the book for weeks, but from the perspective of the rest of us it was only a four-day project. Before we could set our watches, Birdie was yucking it up on Oprah, and the day after that a medical consortium from the Twin Cities telephoned about building a clinic in Cold Beak. Birdie agreed to lend her name to the project, and Barry Larson sold them the same plot on the hill that he had rented to campers on the opening night of The Phoenix. All that happened in the blink of an eye. Time, like the river before it, had flooded its banks, dumping dozens of extra weeks into that one month of July.

Birdie and The Phoenix

On the second day after the phone call, the clinic was built, although the contractor claimed it took months. It was built in the time that it took Jeffrey, Sandy, and Ann to eat their ice cream cones as they stood on a sidewalk below the hill and watched the accelerated blur.

"How'd they do that so fast?" Ann asked.

"Maybe there's a worm hole in the space-time continuum," Jeffrey suggested.

"Mom says don't invent answers that you can't prove," Sandy put in.

"Ish! I hate worms," Ann replied. "Let's go tell Sheriff Maki and get Nut Goodies."

"Let's run!" Jeffrey added, and they did that.

About this time one of the high school students got Ferguson to publish a poem in *The Peep*. I think it was from an old play, and literary types said it was pretty good.

> The time is out of whack.
> Oh cursed spite!
> How can we turn it back?

I guess you have to have read the *Cliff Notes*.

• • •

The Birdella May Borguson Institute for Weight Loss, with its famous Hall of Healing and Hope, brought rich people and their portfolios to Cold Beak, and in the days that followed its remarkable appearance, new homes and businesses popped into existence with equal disregard for the usual laws of temporality. Whether they popped out of worm holes or not will be for the scientists to debate on Hardball, but a lot that might have been vacant as you strolled to work in the morning would be the site

After the Floods

of a sparkling new bank building, all glass and reflecting surfaces, as you trudged home in the afternoon.

Some citizens stood by in awe, clocking the projects with stop watches. In the B.S., Gopher contended with exploding jungles of hair to mow. Hair grew so fast that a single customer might show up two or three times a week. The place was stuffed with garbage bags of hair, and locks drooped over the spittoons and collected in the corners like ivy.

Gopher, assuming an air of expertise, assured frightened clients that time can in fact get out of whack. In his view, it happens when the Earth's magnetic poles are about to reverse themselves. He watches The Discovery Channel. From the pulpits, preachers talked angels and demons, and in the new university, also an overnight wonder, professors talked relativity, frames of reference, and string theory.

Despite the whole time-being-out-of-whack thing, it was clear that Birdie had saved Cold Beak from economic ruin. She flooded the town with energy and optimism, shaking, shimmying, and laughing until God winked down on us and broke the rules, maybe to apologize for the April disaster. Everyone in town lined up at banks with piles of bills to be counted with much laughter and back slapping, and the collection plates were piled high each Sunday with large bills and larger checks.

The outrage of Judgmentalists like Elvira Emerson evaporated like last summer's joke. I even saw Rev. Olson's husband wearing a Birdie Watcher tee shirt in the grocery store. As Homer said, a moral prejudice doesn't have much chance against prosperity; a soap bubble has more shelf life.

Unfortunately, Birdie's vanity grew with her reputation. Exercise had done wonders for her body, and the throne in the cargo area of Homer's pickup was history. Her hair no longer

Birdie and The Phoenix

stuck out like bed springs in six directions. It was darker and had that draped, curvy look. She purchased a pink Cadillac convertible, had "Birdmobile" lettered on the trunk, and wore strange assortments of clothing garnered from Minneapolis's most expensive shops.

She even gave up snoose, and some people said that a little of Ferguson's outlook had found a place in hers. On the steps of the church, folks would part and she'd pass like royalty. Fortunately, her vanity phase didn't last beyond Hulda's tragedy, which was everyone's tragedy too.

Until the tragedy, health was the order of the day. 12 Hour Fitness became 18 Hour Fitness, the jogging path by the river had a steady stream of marathon aspirants, and chinning bars sprouted in back yards. Cold Beak was the unofficial fitness capital of the Upper Midwest.

• • •

Betty enrolled at the Borguson Institute, where Homer often visited her. It cut into his time at the B.S., but he solemnly assured her that she was worth it. It was one of those moments. They would meet by the fountain with its statue of Birdie spouting water from the mouth. Some reports have it that honeymoon plans were made there, as the peacocks patrolled the lawn. I'd have preferred horses, but there's no accounting for taste. Anyway, the honeymoon was to consist of spring-training games and off-shore fishing in Florida, much to Betty's strategically generated enthusiasm. They shared a stick of Juicy Fruit to cap the deal.

Homer's courting was accompanied by his own, private transformation. With the help of the new tanning salon and lots of lotion, he became as brown and creamy as a chocolate fondue, and some folks complained that his cologne made him smell like

After the Floods

a certain newspaper editor. When the word spread about him and Betty, people naturally shared opinions. Since Betty and Birdie were both heavy girls, one fellow at the B.S. volunteered that Homer was wise to stick with a size he was used to.

"It's like with ice cream," the man said. "Once you get used to a flavor, ain't no use in changing."

"Or it's like when you always go to a good fishing hole," Fred suggested, shooing a fly from his nose. "No point driving up every dirt road looking for another."

Alligator was in the B.S. that day and was about to offer his comparison, but Homer roared out, flashing his rubble of teeth so folks would know that he wasn't angry, that any more such talk wouldn't be polite. Usually talking politeness with the B.S. boys was like asking a room full of cats to form a line, but in this case the boys changed course and took to dusting off old tales about fish they'd caught and people they'd met, all shameful lies and brainless flap-doodle.

A Soldier Dies

Well, the town experienced four or five years worth of growth by the end of July, and time began to slip back into its normal alignment, which is to say that events progressed in sync with one another as though they all happened in the same universe. Then Hulda learned, fearing it even as the people in uniform approached her doorstep, that her husband, Jerry, had died. Jerry had been assigned to escort medical personnel to a triage site in the outskirts of Baghdad, and his vehicle had been attacked. A few days after she received the news, the coffin arrived in a hearse from the airport in the Twin Cities.

Birdie and The Phoenix

The family and closest friends gathered around the burial site, but others came to the cemetery as well. It was a warm afternoon, and lovely. Flowers were in bloom on the graves and throughout the town. Nature doesn't adjust itself to suit the occasion, no matter what the old writers say.

The crowd spread itself across the spacious grounds of the cemetery, surrounded the new marble angel, and even flowed onto the street where Sheriff Maki leaned on his car with his hat in his hand. At the edge of a grove on the adjoining land, a peacock stared at us with a hundred eyes. Homer and Oscar, who had both served, were in uniform, and so was I. Rev. Olson presided.

"Knowing that all rivers journey to the sea, and that dust returns to dust, we ask you, O Lord in Your mercy, to accept into Your tender care our courageous friend and our loved one, Gerald Lund. We ask it in the name of the Father, the Son, and the Holy Ghost. Amen."

Even Siiri Elden, who is not a believer, said "Amen," and as the casket was lowered, Rev. Olson sprinkled dust upon it and Oscar played taps. Jeffrey stood quietly, clutching his mother around the waist. Many of us felt new orders of despair and rage flood up from dark places. Those who were the last to say goodbye that day observed a crow swoop low over the new grave, drop a rose upon it, and return to her mate in a tree. Someone said the crow had a tear in its eye. The crow was real, but I think the tear was added as a way for the human imagination to honor a dead friend. Most stories have such touches.

• • •

A week later Mattie and Pete met again in the park beside the river, passing by the tree where the broken robin's egg had been found. Mattie was nervous about the birthday present she had

After the Floods

bought for Pete, because she had not realized at the time that Pete's broken watch was a souvenir of his life with Irene. Nonetheless, the gift was offered.

"This one has a perpetual calendar," she said. "You'll never have to set the date."

Pete opened the box and pondered the watch as mourning doves called to one another and joggers passed on the path with iPods plugged in their ears. Then Mattie suggested a two-watch solution: Irene's ancient gift could be put on a chain and worn around the neck.

"Yes, I'll do that," Pete said. Then, for the time being, he put Mattie's watch on his wrist beside Irene's. The conversation drifted—conversations are so often like clouds—to Mattie's ex, whom Pete understood to have been a lawyer.

"No," Mattie said. "I don't pick them that good, or didn't. He chased ambulances for a lawyer and talked old ladies into suing over every cough or steep stair. In his down time, he was all about bimbos and booze."

"So you left him?"

"No, he left me. I couldn't stand the thought of being pitied by making our problems known, but of course they were known. We think we're keeping secrets, but all the while we're open books. Anyway, when he left with the whore from hell, I went to my sister's place in Arkansas for a while. I got over it, like I got over acne, and then I moved here to be independent. That's why I'm pals with Siiri Elden. I admire her independence."

"I took a trip to the Gulf Coast after Irene died," Pete said. "It was strange driving back into the snow. It was good, but in a solemn way, knowing that I belong where winters are cold."

"There are fireplaces," Mattie reminded him.

Birdie and The Phoenix

"Being homesick is part of getting older. I think substitute homes are never . . ."

"No, they aren't. But you can't just quit. You haven't thought of quitting have you?"

Pete paused for a moment, then said, "That house we had up on the Range just wasn't home anymore." Perhaps it was a way of saying yes, he had thought about quitting. I don't know.

Pete and Mattie stopped in their walk to watch some boys toss a football, and Mattie's mind drifted to Hulda and her difficulties after the funeral, difficulties enhanced by the fact that her father had taken to bed again.

"I feel so sorry for Jeffrey," Mattie said, "the way our government took his childhood right away from him."

"We need to get Jeffrey on the flag-football team," Pete said. "The first scrimmage is Saturday."

"Let's you and me stop by their house," Mattie suggested.

I'm not one to find silver linings in tornados, and I detest attempts to proclaim sweetness and light, or a divine plan, in the brutal death of a young man. But it is true that the mutual decision to help Jeffrey back into his childhood was one of the things that in turn helped Mattie and Pete out of their respective isolations.

• • •

The spike in Cold Beak's economy had resulted in a new recreation center for the children, complete with indoor and outdoor swimming pools and an athletic field, and Pete found his calling working with the kids. He arranged special programs for the children of small people, as well as programs that would bring all the kids together. A number of parents were in the bleachers for

After the Floods

the football scrimmage on Saturday, and Hulda sat with Mattie, Siiri, and Rev. Olson.

There was the inevitable audience of crows on the power line, heckling and cawing. Two crows, perched at a distance from the others, almost seemed to be chatting with each other as their heads bobbed first in Birdie's direction and then at the boys on the field. Of course all eyes, human and avian alike, went often to Birdie, who had re-fashioned her Phoenix costume into a cheerleading outfit. The Clydesdales joined her on the sidelines to do the Funky Chicken and shout encouragement to the Cold Beak Ducks, now divided into a red team and a blue team.

Many noteworthy events punctuated the game: 1) Billy Larson's left shoe came off as he ran after the ball; 2) Mark Husby's pants fell down, causing him to cry; 3) Sandy Elden got a bloody nose and wiped it on his new Ducks jersey; 4) Jeffery Lund intercepted a pass and ran for a touchdown, causing Hulda to 5) stand and shout like a college girl, resulting in 6) Rev. Olson's face blossoming into a smile and 7) Mattie's eye emitting a gentle tear. During a time out Pete was observed to 8) hug Jeffrey vigorously and muss his hair.

That night the Antler's Lounge was packed. Homer and Betty danced, as did the slim girl who was saving money for new boobs. Her partner was one of The Clydesdales. Pete and Birdie worked the bar with much laughter and bravado, and Mattie slid onto a stool beside Oscar and me. Oscar had been telling me about his tour in Iraq and asking me about how I got my Picasso face in Vietnam.

"Hello Lars," Mattie said. "Can we get you to run for mayor again?"

Of course I was being flattered, and of course I loved it.

Birdie and The Phoenix

"Hey bartender!" she called. "What's a girl have to do to get a dance around here?"

Oscar grinned and limped around the bar to take over for Pete. The song on the juke was "Speak Low," which Mattie sang softly as the couple danced.

"I wait, darling I wait.

Will you speak low to me,

Speak love to me, and soon?"

Betty rolled her eyes as Homer spoke low into her ear:

"So it was third and eight, with the Packers down by three. Farve stepped back into the pocket . . ."

I have good hearing, in case you're wondering.

Exit Ferguson

A black Lincoln glided across the Barton Memorial Bridge, swerved to avoid a pothole, and hurried past the water tower before being pulled over by Sheriff Maki, who confronted a black man and a white man in dark glasses and business suits. Mourning doves kibitzed from a power line, sometimes rubbing shoulders and nodding their heads.

"You guys on a mission?" Mike asked.

"Sorry, officer," the black man replied, smiling congenially. "The foot got a little heavy."

Maki produced two Nut Goodies. "I'll trade you these for a look at your driver's license and registration," he said, smiling.

The papers were produced and returned, and Maki reminded the visitors that there would be children playing near the streets and that the speed limit was 30 mph. He also suggested that

After the Floods

the candy wrappers should be disposed of properly. Then Maki walked over to chat with (and chide) Bob Carlson, parked nearby and selling walleyes illegally from an ice chest in his hatchback. Bob has trouble understanding that the rules cover him, too. He requires patience. The Lincoln edged past them and continued its slow drift into town.

"You know what they call the Big Mac in Paris?" the black guy asked. "They call it the Royale."

"Duh," the white guy responded, examining his fingernails.

The car eased into a parking spot in front of *The Weekly Peep*, and the two men stepped out, stretched, and looked around. Across the street, a black child and a white child approached Gopher's B.S., arguing loudly.

"It was an angel dropped the rose," one child was heard to say.

"It was just a crow," the other affirmed.

"A *guardian* crow then."

One of the children pulled a Nut Goodie from a pocket.

"Hey! Where'd you get that?" the other asked.

"I know a guy."

"Sweet."

The Nut Goodie was shared, not quite equally, as the kids stopped to look at Gopher's parrot in the window.

"That's progress," the black man said. "Soon they'll have inter-marriage. They'll have little creamy-mocha kids running around every hick town in the state. The end of milk-white America."

"I wonder if they have a Starbucks," the white guy mused, looking away down the street.

As the two men entered the office, Ferguson stood over the shredder and fed it documents known only to himself.

"You Ferguson?" the black guy asked.

"Yes," Ferguson said nervously. "I hope there isn't a problem, gentlemen. I can assure you that *The Weekly Peep* does its very best to be fair and balanced in all of its . . ."

"We're here to buy you out," the white guy declared. He had a soft, staccato voice like the keyboard of a computer clicking.

"But wait just a minute," Ferguson protested. "You can't just . . ."

"Of course we can," the black guy said.

The strangers were lawyers. After Jerry Lund's funeral, and as if by unspoken agreement, the town had ratcheted up its attention to the welfare of the young. Birdie's book, *Swing and Sway with Birdella May*, had become an overnight best seller, and most people assumed that Birdie had arranged to buy *The Peep* and then give it to Seth Hogan, Ferguson's young assistant. Ferguson was offered a fair price, but the clincher was a five-year contract with the *Minneapolis Star Tribune*, a contract that was also assumed to have strings leading back to the newly rich and influential Birdella May.

"So kid, when you take over this . . . ," the black guy paused, "this rag . . ."

"*The Peep*," the white guy prompted. "They call it *The Peep*."

"*The Peep*, yeah. When you get *The Peep,* change the name, kid. *Peep* sucks."

The lawyers were out of there, leaving Ferguson clutching a handful of legal documents. The Lincoln swerved around potholes and then glided past the water tower and over the bridge.

"Let's get a Big Mac," the black guy said. "Can you get a Royale in the boondocks?"

"Cow," the white guy said. "Let's stop somewhere and eat cow."

In a few days, Ferguson signed and mailed the papers that sold *The Peep* to Seth via the subterranean route named Birdie May.

After the Floods

A Digression on Nut Goodies

For a while when I was a kid, I was mainly Hershey Bars. A Hershey was neatly minted, a perfect rectangle made up of squares that could be broken off one at a time. You didn't just bite into a Hershey, or at least I didn't, you broke off the squares, being careful to leave right angles. The Hershey catered to my fastidious side, the side that didn't want the gravy to get on the peas or the potatoes to touch the meat.

The same was true of the Three Musketeers, with its grooves that allowed, or demanded, equal sharing among three interested parties. Mounds and Almond Joy came as two small bars that didn't even need to be separated by a grimy hand. These bars almost insisted that they be shared.

On the other grimy hand, the Nut Goodie, a lump of milk chocolate with peanuts and a maple paste inside, was (and is) not minted or stamped from a mold. It has no creases or lines, and it doesn't try to teach you to share. A Nut Goodie minds its own business. I imagine it plopped from a certain altitude onto a tray or conveyer belt, where it hardens into a delicious, rocky blob. It is not a bar at all, but a friendly old hill of candy. As with most things that go plop, no two Nut Goodies are exactly alike. From an aesthetic view point, and perhaps a social one as well, it was a rebellious candy, the polar opposite of the fussy, squared-away Hershey.

Getting my head into Nut Goodies was a matter of loosening up my attitudes, breaking free of the rules. Eating a Nut Goodie was like coloring outside the lines. It was the Jackson Pollack of candy bars. If someone asked me to share my Nut Goodie, I intentionally broke off a small piece. Hey, it was my candy. The Nut Goodie taught me that things don't have to be just so. It

74

was a lesson in life. With its amorphous shape, the flavor of the Nut Goodie was the flavor of randomness. I became a new kid, more self-confident, more my own man.

Of course it's different with Sheriff Maki. He shares whole Nut Goodies the way I used to share squares of the Hershey or thirds of the Three Musketeers. But Mike's an adult. He can buy Nut Goodies by the carton and toss an entire bar in Ferguson's lap without thinking twice. He can write them off as a business expense or charge them to the county. I'm talking about the lives of kids back when candy money was scarce and children's property rights were unheard of.

Now back to our story.

Love and Marriage

Prosperity also jump-started the bliss business in Cold Beak, and among the weddings at the Lutheran Church was the two-fer of Betty-and-Homer and Oscar-and-Birdie. Fred and Moose were best men. Fred succeeded for the most part in ignoring his attendant fly, although one of the photos—I gaze at it as I write—caught him slapping at a speck on his left ear. Sometimes I imagine Fred in heaven with a halo of gnats.

After the wedding ceremony, there was a snowstorm of rice as the couples ducked and ran for cars that were well labeled with "Just Married" signs. Tires squealed, and the couples sped out into the world of the blissfully hitched.

Oscar and Birdie went straight to Oscar's hobby farm on the far side of the Institute. Oscar had a few cattle, and he, or they, supplied a local creamery with milk. Beyond that, the farm was mainly a flower garden and some apple trees. It was a good place

After the Floods

to start a family. Homer and Betty decided on a more cosmopolitan honeymoon and spent three days and nights in a luxury hotel in St. Paul, enjoying meals wheeled into their room under glass and served with cloth napkins, all of this being merely a prelude to the glorious two weeks planned for the following year's spring-training adventure in Florida.

It wasn't long before Birdie and Oscar had the whole gang out to the farm for her special vegetarian hot dish. As she explained it, she no longer ate things that had once had mothers. The day was warm, and in the late afternoon people sat in the yard watching the swallows arc about, catching fast food on the fly. The creek in back of the house, which emptied into the New Hope River a mile away, made a soft sound, and the maple leaves in the grass were sheets of gold beat thin.

"So you dumped that pink Cadillac," Homer remarked as they lounged in the yard.

"I'm ashamed of that purchase," Birdie answered. "Anyway, who wants a convertible up here in the winter?"

People knew that she felt regret. Homer made up for his inappropriate remark by offering gum all around, and Gopher kindly changed the subject by observing that it would be a cold winter. June responded that the newspaper had said the winter would be warm, causing Gopher to speculate on whether a statement that your wife doesn't hear is still wrong. Opinions were predictably divided.

Birdie gazed off at a formation of geese in the sky.

"The government sends our children home in coffins, and here I am riding around in a new convertible like the Queen of Sheba."

"Birdie," Betty said, moving closer to hold her hand.

There was a moment of silence, and then Birdie observed

Birdie and The Phoenix

that the cows would be dragging their shadows back to the barn soon, and she was ready to put her hot dish on the table if someone would go and find Ole, who had wandered off toward the creek.

Oscar and Homer walked around the house and leaned on a fence to study Ole, who stood near the creek dabbing his face with his red bandana and looking into the brown eyes of a cow. Swede sniffed around in the grass. Ole stroked the cow's forehead, and when Oscar called him to supper, he kissed the cow on the nose before joining his own kind again. Personally, I'd rather kiss a horse, but that's just me.

Later, as forks clinked and seconds were passed, Oscar announced that by and by Homer would have a nephew or niece. Sometimes when a newly married couple makes such an announcement, folks do some quick math in their heads. Of course there was no point in doing the math in Cold Beak that summer.

• • •

Pete missed the vegetarian hot dish, since the Ducks were having a chalk talk and a cookout at the recreation center. No doubt Pete got in touch with his inner Super Bowl Coach, drawing plays on the blackboard and describing the paths to be followed by blockers and tight ends. And no doubt children inquired about whether there was also a loose end and why do they have to bend over in the huddle anyway. Probably Jeffrey Lund and Sandy Elden followed some of what Pete said, and very likely Billy Larson struggled with a shoe lace. Someone complained that he was thirsty.

The next afternoon Pete and Ole took to the jogging path, along with the trusty Swede, the three of them running more easily than before.

After the Floods

"Homer says you're dating a farm animal."

"She's just a friend," Ole protested. "I live with Swede. I hear you're friendly with Hulda."

"That would be with Jeffrey."

• • •

Mattie and Pete had seen less of one another in recent days, and Mattie, coincidentally, was a bit on edge. That night Mattie worked the cash register at The Phoenix, when Pete came in with the entire Lund family, Hulda, Jeffrey, and the old man, who was apparently on a sabbatical from his bed. As Mattie told it later, she felt it best to slip away discreetly. Other informants claim that her dikes broke, and it was her swift kick that caused Lancelot to deconstruct with an uncourtly clatter.

In any case, she headed into the kitchen and out the back door, where she had the new patio to herself. Eventually Hulda slipped into a chair beside her. The aurora borealis flooded the sky.

"Just think," Hulda said, "there are folks who have never even seen the northern lights."

"Yeah," Mattie said, "like in that song. How are you doing?"

"Good. Pete has been wonderful, helping Jeffrey have a childhood after all."

"Like a brand new father," Mattie said, and then she apologized for saying it. Her anger had ebbed away.

"The new rec center saved Jeffrey, and Pete even got my dad out of bed. Dad goes to the center with Jeff for ping-pong and pool."

They watched the northern lights pulse in the sky beyond the river as though the darkness itself might hold a great, invisible heart. Somewhere an owl wondered *who*.

"Jeffrey and I aren't looking for anyone new, not with Jerry so much in our hearts. Maybe someday it will change."

Birdie and The Phoenix

"You don't have to . . ."

"Oh, I think I do," Hulda said. "I almost passed on Jerry over a silly misunderstanding. I remember staring at that engagement ring. Hope alloyed with fear, that's what an engagement ring is made of. Not every guy is like that ex of yours. You need to give loyalty a chance."

"I'm always . . . getting angry," Mattie said.

"There's Lexapro for that. Listen, women need to help each other in this bottom-up world. I don't know how much you reached out to that ex, and I don't want to know. But I do know that a woman can't just sit by and wait for things to come up roses. Men are like that suit of armor. They need assembly and maintenance. It's that 'value-added' idea."

There would be live music that night in the Antlers Lounge, and it was agreed that Mattie would join Hulda and her family for a few minutes. Once Mattie coaxed Pete onto the dance floor, Hulda and her charges would disappear.

"My dad drove tonight," Hulda said, "which means Pete will need a ride home. Nudge-nudge."

"Say no more," Mattie replied. She had her smile back.

• • •

The slim girl danced with her Clydesdale as Mattie and Pete took the floor. The River Boys, who also worked sometimes at the dance hall in Eveleth, played "Seems Like Old Times."

"Mooo," Mattie said contentedly, resting her head on his chest.

"Me tooo," he replied.

It is rumored that they went on to discuss the size of the family they would have and the immense pleasure involved in reaching that size. Mattie joked that they suffered from the seasonal mating disorder. The slim girl also whispered to her man:

79

After the Floods

"Betty said she'd be a donor. That might be better than silicone . . . more natural."

"Trust me," the gentleman replied, "silicone is the way to go. It's been thoroughly tested."

"You care about my boobs," she sighed, dropping her head on a large pec. "That's nice."

"I only want what's best for you."

In a tree outside, the owl continued to ask *who*. The stork above the front door was as pleased with the evening's events as a stork made of wood could be. Other birds throughout the town and along the river tucked their heads under wings of various colors among canopies of leaves high above the ground. Frogs croaked in ponds, and crickets chirped. Swede, at home by the fireplace, drooled in his sleep. It was a typical late-summer night in Minnesota.

Life Goes On

On a Sunday afternoon in the fall, Pete and Jeffrey sat in front of the TV with elevated feet and Cokes in hand, watching the Vikings play the Packers. It was a week or two after all the trouble with Saint Bob and the Sowers at the hospital, trouble that I won't go into here since it was in all the papers and you probably know about it. Anyway, the Sowers were arrested, and things settled back into their normal grooves fairly quickly.

"The Vikings can't find their bottoms with flashlights," Pete said. "The quarterback wears lace panties."

Jeffrey giggled and replied that the Vikings' coach drives an old Ford pickup from the Iron Range, whereupon some spirited sofa-wrestling ensued.

Birdie and The Phoenix

Out back, in Mattie's garden, Mattie and Hulda pulled carrots and picked tomatoes for the evening's salad.

"I've been worrying about Jeffery's future," Hulda said, examining an especially large carrot that the ground had finally relinquished.

"You're doing a great job with Jeffrey," Mattie replied. "I'm sure things will work out."

Hulda wiped her face with a sleeve, giving her nose an exotic smudge. "But if something should happen to me?" she asked, tapping dirt off the carrot. "I don't have any relatives left around here."

Mattie thought for a moment. "I'll see to it that Jeffrey is fine. We'll take care of Jeffrey." And then, after another moment of silence, she added, "And if something happens to me, you could keep an eye on Pete . . . if you're free."

It was halftime for the Vikings, and as Pete and Jeffrey looked out the window into the garden, the women touched one another affectionately and Mattie wiped the dirt from Hulda's nose. One of the crows in the apple tree whispered something to its mate.

"Are they crying because Mom got dirt on her nose?" Jeffrey asked.

"It must be a girl thing," Pete said. "They're fine. Wanna go out and see?"

Jeffrey dashed for the back door. "Last one out is a Viking!" he shouted.

• • •

Ferguson's very first assignment with the *Star Tribune* was to fly to New York, take in a play, and wax wise about it in print. He was stepping into the glittering future of his dreams, and as he sat in the airliner with his trophy blonde at his side, his imagination reached out to even greater triumphs, to luncheons with Tom

After the Floods

Stoppard and vacations with Brad and Angelina. These gauzy visions were interrupted by his companion, who wanted to know what in God's name *The Boob Dialogues* would be about.

"We'll find out tomorrow night," Ferguson replied. "It's by a Minneapolis woman with a feminist ax to grind into art."

"Maybe I'll see *Cats*," the lady replied, "and join you afterwards at the party where you said we'd meet Tom Stopper."

"*Cats* closed years ago. Stoppard, his name is Tom Stoppard. He writes plays."

"Ooooh!" she exclaimed in her little, squealing way derived from old movies. "Does he write plays about house pets? I want us to have lots of house pets. Maybe there's a play about puppies that I can see tomorrow."

Ferguson suppressed a sigh, and then came the flight attendant's announcement about upright tray tables, locked positions, and seat belts. Through the window, Ferguson could almost hear the lights of New York whisper their promises. I trust that he was pleased to no longer live in a town where people judge you by what you are.

• • •

As autumn moved toward winter, all in a swirl of falling leaves and ambling clouds, Pete and Mattie officially became a couple. Often they spent evenings with Ole before withdrawing together to Mattie's house, where I imagine each was like a happy child gazing into the secret heart of a rose.

In these delicate matters, though, omniscient narration (if the cobbling together of rumors and speculations can be called omniscience) must wear the blinkers of decorum, so let us mind our own nocturnal beeswax and remain with Ole and Swede, lying on a thick carpet before a fire. Perhaps Ole sipped chocolate from

Birdie and The Phoenix

his Birdie mug, and it is likely that Swede was still digesting the weekly news. Under Seth it had become *The Cold Beak Beacon,* and Swede irreverently chewed it to pulp at every opportunity.

Thoughts about the flood and about Birdie's miraculous mission in Cold Beak tumbled through Ole's head, as well as thoughts about his brother's loss on the Iron Range and his new-found happiness with Mattie. The memories and hopes were like a river, laughing and rolling in Ole's mind, softening the lonely places. Or at least I hope so. And the embers in the fireplace were like the lights of a city that you see coming over a hill at night, a city down in a valley glowing with dreams, a cluster of separate dreams that add up to one great dream.

• • •

It requires effort to socialize during the winter, but on warm evenings the ice rink at the recreational complex was a meeting place. Birdie, given her pregnancy and her inexperience with skates, stayed indoors sipping coffee, but many of the others I've told you about glided around the oval plane of ice under blue lights as music drifted from speakers. Few things are more beautiful than snowflakes illuminated by lights beneath the vast darkness, snowflakes descending on children who duck and dodge among the adults, forever losing and finding one another as they call "Marco" and "Polo."

The Wanderers

The Crow Road

Often, on flights to the New Hope River, George and Ruby gazed down and marveled at the statue of a person with wings standing in the middle of the cemetery. Later, hunting nuts or berries near the jogging trail, they would discuss the strange image. Perhaps it was built to scare away birds such as themselves. They had seen such contraptions in gardens, ridiculous assemblages of sticks and cloth meant to stand between them and a brunch of berries or corn. But not far from the winged statue was a birdbath, so the scarecrow interpretation made no sense.

Moreover, the marble statue had an altogether different feel than the silly structures people erected in strawberry patches. It was elegant and brooding, evoking awe rather than fear. Still, Ruby and George agreed that a human capable of flight would be a bad turn of events, a catastrophe from an avian perspective.

"If people evolve into birds," Ruby declared, "you can kiss city life goodbye for the rest of us."

"They'd be too big to sit on phone lines," George mused. Total agreement did not come easy to him.

"But still . . ." Ruby let the topic drop.

One day George and Ruby landed by the cemetery to watch people walk slowly among the monuments and around the statue and then stand solemnly as a box was lowered into a hole.

After the Floods

Later, workmen filled the hole with dirt. The crows decided to make the cemetery their place to rest. Something in the winged statue seemed to invite them, and the birdbath was a plus too. They returned in the evening to nestle among the leaves and branches of an ancient elm.

The following day they set to building a nest, and Ruby was as happy as springtime itself. They would stop being wanderers. The sunlight smelled lush and green, and when they rested they felt like chicks wrapped in summer's golden wings. George was energized, almost his old self again, and they talked through the dawn about materials and design. Would yarn be better than string? Old twigs give a pleasant, rustic effect, Ruby said, but George argued that new twigs are stronger and more pliable.

"Maybe we could have a sort of double or two-room nest in case we want to have guests," Ruby said.

"Crows don't have guests," George pointed out. "It would be unnatural."

The nest was finished in three days, built from all of the materials they had discussed and others that had presented themselves as they scavenged in alleys and back yards. The first night together in their new home would be magical, and in the late afternoon Ruby felt an old, electric thrill pulsing through her feathers as they entered the branches of the tree. The tombstones stretched away into the darkening cemetery like a city without lights, reminding ruby of New Orleans after the storm.

Then, as the darkness moved like water among the monuments below and the moon was a child's balloon caught in the leaves above, a shape rose from a mound that stretched away from a new stone. The shape seeped upward from the soil and was vague like mist, but with the form of a person. It was what remained of an old man, and it moved one way and then

The Wanderers

another near the mound of dirt as though in a shifting breeze. Finally it sat on the mound and slowly vanished.

Another evening produced the shape of a young woman that drifted among the stones and monuments for a week, finally growing less substantial as when a shadow lightens beneath thinning clouds. Now, in the darkening of the day when the bugle had been played and Ruby had dropped the flower, they saw a third form billow up from its mound.

"Maybe we can talk to him," Ruby whispered, leaning close to George on the branch. George cocked his head this way and that. A rising moon came in small pieces between the leaves.

Somewhere, an owl asked its timeless question.

"You," George said to Ruby. "I talk bad." George had become a crow of fewer and fewer words, and those were not always clear. It was a speech problem that came and went. Perhaps he'd had a stroke. It was a sadness for Ruby. *We're getting old*, she thought. *We are going the way of all crows.*

"I'll just alight on the stone near his mound," Ruby said. "I won't be gone long. Don't you go anywhere, darling. You stay right here. Okay?"

"Okaw," George replied.

As Ruby planed down and landed, the mist turned. There was something like a face in it that looked at her, a vague face as from a dream. Then there were thoughts in her head that were not her own, and she knew that the mist was talking to her without sound. She also knew that it was crying. *Maybe they are not made of mist but of tears,* she thought. *Maybe tears are all that is left when they go into the ground.*

Ruby sat for a long time on the stone as the form swayed before her in the breeze, lightened to a glow by the moonlight. His story tumbled like storm clouds in her head. The form in mist was lost,

After the Floods

and Ruby wondered if the winged person in stone was lost too, lost as hawks and even crows sometimes are in their wanderings. Maybe one of the mist people had turned to stone. Far away the owl called again, and here and there small things hurried in the grass, squirrels to their trees and rabbits to their holes.

Ruby returned to the elm to find George dozing.

"It's dead people in the boxes," Ruby said.

"Boxes?" George said, pulling his head languidly from under a wing.

"The boxes they put in the ground when all the people come. It's what they do with dead people. They go into a box, like back into a shell, and then the shell goes in the ground."

"Little houses no?" George asked. He had vague memories of living in New Orleans, where the dead are buried in little houses above ground.

"It's different here."

"Holes are bad."

"The bones stay in the box, and the mist that comes up from the ground is all that is still alive, sort of."

"Sort of alive?"

"I don't know. This one is sad because he was about to come home to see his boy." Ruby paused, remembering her own eggs hurtled from the nest by a storm and smashed on the sidewalk below. *It's too sad, how children and parents are taken away from one another,* she thought. "But then he was made dead and came home in a box and was put in the ground. And now that he is out of the ground, he will go away from life entirely. That's what he said."

"Where do they go?"

"I don't know. He talked about the crow road. What does it mean?"

90

"It's about when they go away," George said, pleased to be able to supply information again.

"It's so strange. They grow up out of the ground like from a seed, but they are just mist that goes away. He wants me to talk to his son. It was hard for him to understand that I can't talk to humans, to living ones."

"But the mist has to go somewhere," George complained, ignoring the question of Ruby talking to the boy. "The crow road has to go somewhere. No road goes nowhere."

"Where does light go when it is gone?"

"I'm going to sleep."

With that, George folded his head carefully under a wing. Despite the brief moment concerning the crow road, his old role of the all-knowing bird was also turning to mist, and Ruby was left to contemplate what the man's mist had said about "forever." *How can there be such a thing?* she wondered. Somewhere a cricket chirruped himself to sleep.

A Caged Bird

The air lightened, and the Corvuses awoke and hunted for nuts on the ground. At night the orange ball had dipped into a vast well of heat to the west, and now it floated up from the edge of things and began to spill the heat. The crows visited the birdbath. They took their morning flight and eventually found themselves gazing down from the roof of *The Weekly Peep*. Large, bulky clouds had moved in, and eventually it would rain. Ruby contemplated the parrot in the cage beyond the lettered window of the barber shop.

"When they come out, their hair is shorter," she remarked.

After the Floods

"Caw?" George asked.

"They want their hair just so. It's a place for the men to get their hair just so. The women go to a different place. We've met birds who are like that about their feathers."

"Why is the parrot kept there?"

"I think they just like to have him there."

"Trapped?"

"Yes," Ruby said, "trapped."

A mockingbird, the same one they had observed soiling the statue and the bath in the cemetery, settled on the roof of the barber shop and then took flight again as though suddenly remembering something. It was a bird Ruby disliked, arrogant and brimming with sarcasm, always making fun of George's speech. *And stay away*, she thought as the bird disappeared behind the hardware store.

Cars bumped and rattled on the street, and people came from buildings carrying bags. A large, black car parked beneath them. Two children approached the barber shop and stopped to look at the parrot in the window. They had candy bars, and one of them put her nose on the glass and tapped it with a finger.

"They frighten the parrot," George said.

"They're young," Ruby replied. "They don't understand." But a slight fear went through her at the thought that they might grow wings like the statue in the cemetery.

"Maybe the parrot comes out at night like mist," George said. Words came to him more easily that day, and Ruby was happy.

"It's strange how they put things in cages, boxes, and bags" Ruby mused. "Everything inside of something else. It's like shells. Everything has a shell."

"Where do the cages and bags come from?"

"I don't know," Ruby answered. "Boxes?"

The Wanderers

As the children turned away from the window, the girl dropped a green and red piece of paper, wiped her hands on an old skirt, and then looked up at Ruby and smiled. Her eyes were small petals on a sunlit pool. Then a feathered child approached Ruby and George, sinking and surging with each stroke of its wings, and landed on the roof near Ruby.

"Bon jour! Je suis Thomas and I come from France but now I live here since we dropped upon a freighter and then upon a choo-choo because we're magpies and we don't hunger to fly so much so much but we just must come to Cold Beak since everyone's doing it doing it and we are so joyfilled here to walk upon zah ground and to, how you say? to peek? no to peck for nuts and bugs and sometimes we fly to zah cow pasture for a peeknic. We sit on backs of cows and peek, no peck, at bugs in zah fur, do you say fur? It's fun to ride on a cow and I pretend that a cow is a sheep no ship and I'm Jack Sparrow zah Pirate which are people I like a lot a lot. We live across zah cemetery from you and we see you often chez vous in your tree and each time Momma say you are Corvuses and we are Corvidaes and so relatives from a long time ago ago. I must ago now to meet my brother who is Paul so we can make play until he bump me by mistake and I cry and Momma scold him how she does say-ing la-la . . ."

The child's voice trailed off in the air as he dipped and surged over the roof of Homer's Ace Hardware.

"I'm hungry," George said, watching young Thomas vanish in the distance.

"We could fly to the park by the river and find nuts," Ruby replied, "but first I'm getting that piece of paper." During Thom-as's monolog, she had kept her eye on the paper dropped by the human child in front of the barber shop. "You wait here."

After the Floods

"I want a mouse . . . or a frog," George declared when she returned with the candy wrapper.

Sometimes George accepted Ruby's call for a vegetarian diet, and on these occasions Ruby smiled at the thought that George was evolving. But at other times the ancient instincts surfaced.

"George, we're too old for frogs and mice," Ruby said, or tried to say through the paper clutched in her beak. "We're becoming civilized."

To George, becoming civilized was a fearful prospect, like becoming deranged. At the far end of Main Street, gulls gathered in the parking lot of the drive-in restaurant, their squeals sounding somewhere between a choir of pigs and an orchestra of kazoos. They made it hard to discuss civilized dining.

"What if I see a mouse that's already dead?" George asked.

"Okay," Ruby sighed.

They stopped at their secret tree to deposit the candy wrapper, and then they flew to the river, alighting in a birch tree near the path where the people run. Two men and a large dog panted on the bank of the river, one of them flapping his arms back and forth along the grass as though trying to fly.

"They'll scare the frogs away," George complained.

"If they can be scared, they're not dead. If they're not dead, we don't eat them."

"This diet is killing me," George said. "I'm shriveling to a moth."

"You look great, George. You look young again."

"Caw?"

"Caw."

The Wanderers

Beyond the Wind

In the distance, at the bottom of a slope, a machine struggled across a field, muttering as the long grass fell behind it.

"Its sound smells tired," Ruby said.

"Do you still smell sounds?"

"Sometimes. I hear colors, too. They hum little tunes."

The crows had flown across the river to explore, and now George dozed beside his wife on a branch. Ruby watched nervously as a bald eagle floated above the far end of the field. It dipped quickly to the ground and then flew off with something clutched in its talons. She was glad that George hadn't noticed. *So much violence*, she thought.

In New Orleans she had not understood where human food comes from, but the trip north had been educational. Now she knew that the cattle kept on farms are killed for food and that birds are shot for food or just for fun. It amazed her how humans were just like animals but then again, with their cars and tall buildings, not at all like animals. Also, people kill each other for reasons that would baffle an animal, as she had been baffled by the mist in the cemetery who had tried to explain war. She understood fighting for food or territory, but religion and pride? What were they?

She wondered why they had left New Orleans. It had been such a long flight, much longer than any they'd taken before, and it had been hard for George, who often wandered off course and needed to stop every couple of miles. Whoever coined the phrase "as the crow flies" didn't have George in mind. "Crows don't migrate!" had been his constant refrain, and they had spent a night on top of a truck parked by the road because he was too tired to fly another inch.

95

After the Floods

Once, crossing a lake in Iowa with George's wings laboring to maintain altitude in a wind shear, she had thought that he would simply fold up and drop into the waves. Perhaps it is wrong to reach too far. Perhaps falling in the waves is the price you pay. Humans had an old story about it.

"My wings are feathered bricks!" George shouted.

Before George could collapse, she landed on a dock where rowboats were tied. George stumbled to a stop behind her and lay there panting for what seemed like an hour, the cold water lapping up between the boards of the dock. Ruby had once heard that there is a special providence in the fall of a sparrow. She wondered if it is true of crows as well. But why would anyone plan the fall of a sparrow or a crow? What's so special about that?

Lately, George had been complaining about headaches and sore joints. *He won't make it back to New Orleans*, Ruby thought now, huddled by him a mile from Cold Beak, Minnesota. She remembered how vibrant George had been so long ago, coming to her all in a rush of feathers and flesh in so many small places of sticks, string, and straw—in Audubon Park, along the levee, or in an old magnolia tree in a yard on Laurel Street. Now there'd be no more eggs.

A large, black car whispered along the road, and the poplar leaves fluttered like small, brilliant wings until the sun went behind the far trees, dipping toward the black well to fill itself with more heat. The leaves of trees were turning yellow, orange, and red. The tractor left the field, and then clouds appeared further off. It was the quiet time before darkness comes smelling of soft feathers as it settles through branches and over fields.

Then trees on the side of the field opposite the road began to move, nodding and turning to one another as though a serious issue had arisen among them. Their colorful leaves tumbled together and apart. Ruby knew that they would move the air in their excitement, and soon the trees near her became agitated as well. Branches rose and fell, whispering loudly and making the air swirl. From another tree, a flock of red-winged blackbirds exploded into the air and shrunk to cinders over the field. The light in the air began its liquid slide toward evening.

"We should fly back to our tree in the cemetery," Ruby said. "It'll be dark soon."

"I suppose so," George replied, awaking slowly from his nap and yawning. "But let's stop at the storage tree on the way. I want to see how our stuff is doing."

Ruby glided easily from the branch, and George lifted himself stiffly into the air behind her. He'd let her carve a path. Beneath them, the river flowed southward. Ruby had seen people riding in homes on the water, and she wondered if birds could build nests that would float down the river to New Orleans. George complained of a sore wing as he was buffeted by the increasing wind. Ducks in close-order drill glided smoothly by.

"Bastards!" George muttered. "I'd like to ruffle their plumage!"

Then they alighted by the fallen tree in the grove near the cemetery. It was an area that the people didn't take care of. Peacock feathers had fallen here and there, and tall grass wrapped itself around fallen branches. *The fallen branches of time,* Ruby whispered to herself. They could be words in a sad song, although she had given up on learning to sing.

Where a tree trunk had split, there was a hole in which they hid their things. Ruby pushed her head in first, as George stood aside listlessly. It was growing darker now, and the wind was cold.

"I think it's all here," she said. "Come and see."

George made his way slowly into the hole in the tree and sat down among their treasures, away from the wind. There were

After the Floods

two golf balls, a diamond ring, many bottle caps, a charm from a child's bracelet, aluminum foil, a screw, a quarter, scraps of paper, and a collection of feathers. He nudged a few of the things with his beak in the darkness. *That statue in the cemetery could not have heavier wings than mine*, he thought. Ruby came to sit beside him.

"Do you remember when we found this one?" she asked, picking up the charm. "It was such a lovely afternoon, just a few days after we arrived here. We took it as an omen. We were so happy that day!"

But she knew that George would not remember.

"I'll sleep here tonight," George said, "with our stuff."

"It isn't safe, George. We can't sleep on the ground. There are foxes."

"You sleep on a branch," George said, "I'll be . . ."

In his mind he finished the sentence, but he knew that sound was not forming in his throat. His beak and then his other parts were no longer willing to move. Now he knew how a fire feels when it goes out.

He was quiet among the things they had found and hidden from the wind and the world. Ruby felt something deep and cold flooding her heart, and she wondered if George would be mist when the darkening of the air was complete. And where would the mist go? The air smelled of yesterday. Inside her, a voice said that all of our feathers are autumn leaves.

Billy in the Shade

Cold Beak Trim

To: God
From: Billy Boichild
CC:
Re: Hair

Yo, God. I'm Billy, the latest eruption from that gene vat with the dependable Boichild label. You probably have notes on us on Your hard drive. Hey, You're probably omniscient. But just in case:

The Boichilds bubbled up in the seventeenth century when Charles II flitted back from France to party on like Garth in England, shooing those prune-faced Puritans away with his hanky. Remember? His Flounciness had a few Boichilds in tow—a gaggle of groupies, fops, and other wackjobs in lace and tights. I know, because my grandfather wrote a family history, *The Boichild Chronicles*. It's bound in leather—way cool.

According to Gramps, "child" was an Anglo substitute. In Paris we were the Boisomethingelses. You could find it in Your records. Gramps was only human. For him, the Boichild river, winding back through generations of American importers and British actors, vanished in England at the Restoration, plunging out of history and into the Cirque de Soleil of myth.

I was begat by Barbara and Tony Boichild in Baptist Hospital,

After the Floods

City of New Orleans, Orleans Parish, State of Louisiana, February 26, 1984. Dad and Mom were December and May, and I'm sure Pop was proud that he could still . . . well, You know. My official name is Norman, which was my Dad's idea, but Mom called me Billy right from the opening tantrum (mine).

There's a picture of me in the hospital, a squinting loaf of Billy-dough wrapped in a towel. Once I was wobbling about the house on rubbery legs, I enjoyed a "cute-as-a-bug's-butt" phase that promptly morphed into a "couldn't-we-put-him-on-eBay?" phase (if they had eBay then, which I don't know). But Tony and Barbara bit the parenting bullet and kept me, thank you Jesus. Eventually, I slogged through the Okefenokee of adolescence, emerging on the far end as a detective for the Lord (You), working the streets and oyster bars of The Big Sleazy.

My dad, Tony, owned a furniture store on Canal Street. It imported stuff for snobs in the Garden District, English stuff and French stuff, stuffed stuff and carved-wood stuff. Mom was blasted into the necrocosm three years ago compliments of breast cancer, and Dad's an old guy by himself now. This whole idea of going to heaven is really nice of You, but most of us have issues with the methods of transportation. Cancer's harsh. Cancer bites a big one. I don't mean to criticize.

I mentioned my ancestors because I know You like that who-begat-whom stuff, but I really want to talk about my cruise on the river of righteousness and how the ship docked here, in Minnesota. I don't know what to do next, and I figure if I talk about it You could email some answers. If You're not online, You'll know about my messages to You anyway, and You could encrypt some advice in the clouds or something. I'm not playing the Spiritual Emergency card here, but some advice would be cool.

· · ·

Billy in the Shade

I live a hundred yards off a county road and three miles from Cold Beak, on the other side of the New Hope River. On the county road near my turn off, there's a boxy little church with peeling paint and a steeple like a tent peg. People go there to play born-again bingo on Wednesday evenings. I came here to be reborn too, only in a different way. But I still feel like the same, bumbling Billy of my Bible days.

I thought it would be a hoot, after New Orleans, to scope out the North, to light out for the territory like Huck Finn, only backwards. I drove a car instead of a raft, stayed in motels, and didn't have a black guy with me. Okay, forget the Huckleberry part. There's no "territory" left anyway.

There's a time in a young dude's life, even a devil-may-care Christian like me, when You have to mope on the sidelines (maybe You and Your Son could do some catching up) and let the Mirror call the plays. Well, I'm in the Mirror Phase right now, probably because of how You did such a good job of coaxing spring out of the hills and trees around Cold Beak now that the flood has crept back into the river.

What was that flood about? Were you teed-off? Did someone eat the wrong apple? Never mind. Don't get offended, but I'm not into theological stuff right now. At times like this it's the Mirror that a guy prays to in the morning and again before sleep.

The Mirror Phase isn't about vanity. It's about deep stuff: who am I? where does time go? where do the girls hang out?

What I'm saying is, life has changed. I'm out of New Orleans and pretty much alone. The future's got no more shape than mist in the valley. So I'm checking the Mirror. The Mirror wonders why my eyebrows have grown down to my cheeks. It says I'm white and pasty, with blotches like an omelet. It says if I continue to cut my own hair I'll be locked away and studied by

After the Floods

science. And my coffee-stained sweatshirts have to go. My teeth have to be cleaned or they'll go.

So I took advice from the Mirror and drove to town for a haircut. I'd still like to get some advice from You, too. I'm betting You're just as good as Dr. Phil.

So keep in touch, Dude. I like the clouds as a place for You to scribble Your message.

• • •

It's on Main Street, right next to Homer's Hardware Store, and it's called Gopher's Barber Shop. Bolted to the wall by the door is one of those old barber poles with the red and white stripes spiraling down. The red represents blood, because people went to the barber in the old days to be bled in order to cure what ailed them.

I know, because according to Grandpa's *The Boichild Chronicles* a lot of Boichilds were bled in the seventeenth century. Bleeding supposedly cured insanity, although I figure it probably just mellowed people down by making them tired. Anyway, Gopher's enterprise carries on the ancient tradition metaphorically. Sure, there's the occasional nick to the neck or chin, but the bleeding is usually more about information than about red and white cells.

I sat on an old, fake-leather sofa in front of a well-shuffled pile of magazines—*Field and Stream, Bait and Trap,* and *Maim and Kill* (just kidding)—waiting for Gopher to finish putting white walls on a ginormously fat guy with a radish nose. A cage with a parrot dangled by the window. Of course I didn't know, as I thumbed through pictures of bass jumping, that the barber's name was Gopher, but that was cleared up after the big guy exited with a small notebook protruding from a back pocket and I slid into Gopher's workspace in front of a cracked mirror.

104

Billy in the Shade

"Yup," he affirmed, flipping the cape around my neck, "there's quite a few guys called Gopher around here. It's because we're the Gopher State."

"Sure it isn't the other way around?"

"Hmm, lemme see . . . No. First it was the little animals, then we got to be the Gopher State, and then guys started callin' each other Gopher. I'm pretty sure. I got a friend everyone calls Minnow. No good reason for that that I can see, him being north of six-three. I'm guessin' folks up here just like small animals and started calling each other by small-animal names."

"Got any Rats or House Flies for customers?" I was in my cute mode.

"I call June, my wife, Little Mouse. Where you from? Me and June were watching *Gone With the Wind* the other night on DVD. You all from Atlanta? Your voice's got Atlanta poured all over it."

"New Orleans, actually. We say y'all."

"Say y'all," the parrot agreed.

Gopher had the electric clipper in his paw, and I told him that I preferred to have my hair cut with a scissors. "I don't like it to get real short on the side," I explained. "I want a sort of combed look all around."

"Well now," Gopher replied, scratching his head. "We usually cut the sides with a clipper here in Cold Beak, shave it right down close. It's the same in all the towns around here. You're the second guy this week who wanted it long. The other guy moved to town to stay with his brother."

"I'd kinda like to stick with my own hair habits this time," I said. "I need to adjust to Cold Beak in stages."

"Well," Gopher replied, accepting my point of view, "we are a long way from Atlanta. Cold Beak ain't the end of the world, but on a clear day you can see it from here."

After the Floods

"It doesn't have to be perfect. Could you just shorten it up a little with the scissors?"

"Sure, but I gotta warn you, I ain't a great barber when it comes to the scissors."

Gopher laughed, put the clippers down, and rummaged in a drawer for a scissors. As he hovered the strange tool this way and that around the side of my head, snipping the air and planning a strategy, I pondered the fate of the famous Boichild sideburns that Grandpa had described in *The Chronicles*.

"You're the guy that lives in Byron Olson's old doublewide out in the woods," Gopher declared once snipping was under way. "Some of the boys were mentioning you the other day. A lot of the boys come in on Saturday, just to catch up on the news. What made you all come up here from Atlanta?"

"Just needed a change of scene," I said. "Actually, y'all is plural. We say it to a group of people."

"I'll be! No one ever told me that. Always thought you all were trying to talk to all the different sides of one person's character, so to speak."

"Nothing that profound."

"That fellow that was just in here, Bob Carlson, I think of him in the plural, and not just on account of his size. Bob can be sweet as a cocker puppy one day and come out growlin' like a lion the next. Why, Sheriff Maki had to slap the cuffs on him just last week over at Moose's Pit Stop, and Carlson hadn't even had but four beers. He gets them beer muscles, like they say. Still, he always donates to the Community Improvement Fund. He's forever writing things in a notebook. Hard to know who the real Carlson is. I guess some things are known only to God and Dick Cheney."

"We used to get beer brains," I confessed, flashing on the old

Billy in the Shade

days at The Maple Leaf, a saloon in the University District in New Orleans.

"You drink much?"

"Drink much?" the bird repeated.

"I've cut back."

"Well, that's a good thing," Gopher affirmed. "Carlson, he come up here to Cold Beak all by himself a few years back, just like you. Except he only came from St. Paul. Got himself in some trouble down there after he smacked his wife a few good ones. It was the beer's fault. So he come up here with just the things he could toss on a Greyhound, just the few pieces left of his life. Arrived all by himself on a cold day in January. Now he's the janitor over at the school, only they call him a maintenance engineer to his face."

He paused to gaze out the window, probably recreating for himself the image of Bob Carlson climbing down from the bus with his life in a bag.

Next he asked, "You got some sort of problem you're getting over? For people getting over problems, I always recommend fishing. You should buy some gear at Homer's Hardware and go fishing. Carlson caught him one of the biggest walleyes I ever seen last year. Brung it in the barber shop for everyone to admire. Thought we oughta keep it on display for a few days, even wanted to have a sign made up."

Gopher shook his head and punctuated his description of Carlson with occasional grunts. He filled a minute of silence with a flurry of snips, and then he finished the Carlson story.

"He figured shellac would keep it fresh until he got around to cleaning it, for crying out loud," he said, shaking his head sadly. "Of course he's learned a lot about fish since then. Now he smokes trout." Gopher went silent over some task at the back

After the Floods

of my head, and I tried to imagine Carlson rolling a trout joint. "But I shouldn't be talking so much," Gopher concluded. "A barber has a lot of secrets he needs to keep. It's tough sometimes."

Poor man, I thought, a life of secrets, and all that hair on the floor, too.

"You could dig a hole and whisper the secrets into the ground," I suggested, remembering an old story about secret donkey ears from Introduction to Mythology.

"Never heard of that before."

"It's an ancient cure for the barber's burden. King Midas's barber discovered it."

"Is that a fact? But I gotta admit, it's sort of fun to tell the shellac story to real people."

"I understand," I said. "Polyurethane is best, everyone knows that. By the way, what does 'crine out loud' mean?"

"Oh, that's just an expression. It don't mean much of anything. You ain't one of those religious-cult types, are you?" Gopher asked, coming out of the blue. "Folks have been wondering."

"How did you know?" I asked, thinking *busted!*

Gopher laughed. "Nah, I know you ain't a Sower, cuz the Sowers don't come in here for haircuts. They get their women to cut their hair for free. And they don't talk like you. You must of seen some of them though, livin' out where you do."

I said that I knew nothing about the Sowers.

"Oh, you will. You can mark my words on that! I'm thinking you oughta move into town and get acquainted with sane folks. Now then, is that enough hair on the side? Looks weird to me, seeing a guy climb out of the barber chair with hair showin' on the side. But I'm willin' to bend the rules for a stranger from Atlanta. Just sit there one more minute. Those eyebrows are spooking the kids."

Billy in the Shade

I felt the scissors scuttling about above my eyes. Then, while my eyes were still closed and before I could protest, Gopher's fragrant fingers gouged my scalp with an oily chemical from a green bottle that he'd grabbed on the sly. Once on my feet, I paid him the eight dollars called for by the hand-printed sign taped to the cash register. When I offered another dollar, Gopher merely contemplated it.

"Is there some kind of bribe you're doing here?"

"In Atlanta they call it a tip. They didn't tip in *Gone With the Wind*?"

"This here's Cold Beak. You can tip a couple of quarters over at Martha's Pies, but no one ever tips at the barber shop. It's not like I'm an employee, you know."

Sensing wounded pride, I apologized.

"Okay, I'll drop this dollar off with Alice at Martha's Pies." Alice was a brown-haired blur of a woman who waited tables for the omniabsent owner.

"Good to meet you, Gopher."

"Mind if I call you all Alligator then?"

"Sometimes we say *all y'all* so as to be sure to cover every inch."

Gopher laughed. "If you decide you want a real haircut, come back tomorrow. No charge. I allow 24 hours for buyer's remorse."

I said goodbye to the bird. A few clouds were clumping up in the west, but it was sunny in Cold Beak and the air was crisp and clean. Across the street, a row of crows, imitating a gang of shadows, looked down from the newspaper office. I was young, I was healthy, and thanks to Gopher's lotion I smelled oh so much better than Pledge. Maybe I *was* being born again, and I wondered if the life I was finding in Cold Beak would be the way to live. Maybe I'd have it "made in the shade," as Dad used to say.

109

After the Floods

I drove back to my lair with the window down, enjoying the cool spring air and the Jesus rock on the radio. Birds were everywhere, many that didn't usually live around here. It was like the world's bird reservoir had opened right over Cold Beak. Toward dark a soft rain fell, tiptoeing through the branches and leaves.

• • •

I know You're busy with global warming and things, and when I went back to my place in the woods after the haircut I discovered someone online named Sister Ann. I'm all wireless now. She listens to problems and gives advice, and I signed up for three months with her, using my credit card (thanks, Dad) on her secure site. So I hope You won't mind if I email her, too. Are second opinions okay? Maybe it can be like You're Santa Claus and she's one of Your helpers. Or an angel. Okay?

P.S. Is it true that we get harps in heaven? Can I have a guitar instead? Gibson, please.

A Kid Says Billy's Dumb

To: God
From: Billy Boichild
CC: Allah
Re: Naming of birds and trees

Whassup, God? It's been five days since my haircut, and I took a walk this morning because the flood is finished and spring is finally here like a friend who missed a flight. It was harsh living in the woods all winter, but You did good inventing spring. We owe Ya.

Billy in the Shade

As You know, I blew New Orleans last September, after things in the Apostolic Network went toadmeat. I tossed my gear into a few boxes and bags, like my clothing and video cam, pumped unleaded into the Civic, and pointed it north to follow the gourd. Escaping slaves in the old Underground Railroad were told to follow the drinking gourd, since the North Star is the tip of the gourd's handle. Not that I was a slave. Just a dork.

The Bible is packed with wanderings and sojourns, tight as Lincoln Logs. That's one way Your opus reflects the lives of dudes like me as well as the lives of peoples like the Africans and the Jews. It's really clever how You put those different levels in, all fractal. My own diaspora plopped me into my first winter—my first shovelful of snow, my first parka, my first frostbite (compliments of the wind from the edge of the world), and my first starry night when I figured, thanks to a busted space heater, that my virile young balls might actually freeze solid as rusty old lug nuts.

I live three miles outside of North Cold Butt, across the Barton Memorial Bridge and down a gravel road shaded by a zillion trees. Did I mention this before? Okay, the town is Cold Beak. I drove into town from time to time in the winter when my driveway and the county road were cleared. I rent from the owner of a Mobile station on the edge of town, and he was dude enough to plow my driveway once in a while.

Now that spring has turned up the heat, we have a zillion birds around here in the zillion trees. I guess I said that already. The road to my trailer is lined with feathers of every make and model. In the winter, though, it was mainly owls. All along the road there were owls in the trees and on the utility poles. Canadian owls were the big news, front page coverage in *The Weekly*

After the Floods

Peep. There was a rodent shortage in Canada, and the owls had beaten their way down here looking for nabs.

It was odd to see them perched in the trees with cocked heads, as though America was a weird thing to see. They had come south and I'd gone north, although I wasn't sure what I was looking for. Another difference between me and the owls, my story hadn't moved from Gopher's Barber Shop to *The Peep*. Maybe I'd have been news if the Saturday crowd at the barber shop had caught me munching a juicy rat.

I rent my doublewide for nearly nothing, a generous supply of rodents included. So I'm a fast-food stop for the owls, but my sympathy is more with the little guys on the ground. In the winter, as icicles grew everywhere like fangs, I'd see small tracks in the snow disappearing into bushes, four delicate toes and the wobbling line left by a small tail trailing between the feet. I took to putting cheese bits by my door, and finally I bought a book to help me identify animals by their tracks. My invisible neighbors, whose markings in the snow looked like drawings from Japan, may have been long-tailed shrews.

April here is like cold dishwater spilled everywhere with a few suds still hanging on, and they tell me that's true even in the years the river doesn't flood. It's always gray, the clouds lumbering by like old men in overcoats. When the sun is shining, my little yard only gets about an hour of it. The rest of the time it's shadows of trees doing their daily tug-of-war from opposite sides.

Now it's May and the snow and flood are gone. You see deer tracks in the mud everywhere, and deer themselves. They hang out in what passes for my yard, and they plunge away into the underbrush when I open the door. The last thing you see is the white undersides of their tails. I think of chorus girls exiting.

Billy in the Shade

Also, an occasional black bear mopes around. They aren't gi-mungous like the brown bears in other parts of the country, and usually they aren't mean, just grumpy. They raid garbage cans, and you wait politely until they finish. There are people like that in New Orleans. Can we talk about that sometime, like when You're not busy getting spring started?

• • •

I walked to town yesterday, following a well-shaded creek to the New Hope River and then crossing the bridge in the bright sun. A wind had torn through during the night, and a lot of branches were down. The Gulf Coast has its hurricanes, but up here you can get straight-line winds of a hundred miles an hour that make shingles from roofs fly around like playing cards. And there are tornados. But the night before last, according to my radio, the wind had been a mere sixty miles an hour.

In New Orleans, I was a city kid who never learned the names of birds and trees, so yesterday when I came to a boy tossing rocks in the creek, I asked him the name of the birds I was hearing.

"Strike one!" he exclaimed as one of his pitches landed in an eddy upstream. Then he turned toward me, sized me up, and replied. "First, Mom makes me tell everyone that most of what I say isn't true. It goes back to this car accident we were in that knocked the truth right out of us. So, those are chickadees, mister. Mom says that they call out their own names—chicka-dee-dee-dee."

I listened for a moment and told him that, sure as bear pooh, that's what they were saying.

"Bear pooh!" he scoffed.

"And what kind of trees are these all along the river that the chickadees are camped in?" I asked, rolling with the punch.

After the Floods

The kid gave me a long, baffled look, like he didn't know where to start. He was probably about eleven years old, wrapped in the usual kid uniform of backward baseball cap, baggy pants, and brand-name sneakers.

"Birds don't camp, they perch. And this ain't no river, it's a creek. Ain't you ever seen a real river? The Barton Bridge crosses a real river." He tossed a rock into the water in mock disgust, a not-quite-disguised smile on his face. "Strike two!" he said, giving me the side-eye.

"Is the Mississippi River where it starts in Itasca Park a river or a creek?" I asked. He squinted at me, as though sizing up an adversary. "Never mind," I said, "let's get to the rest of my stupidity. Whadya call those trees?"

"Well, if you want to believe me those are poplars, but when you're in Colorado you can call them aspen. Where you from, anyhow? You some kind of Southerner?"

I acted frightened and gave a worried look around. "You ain't gonna tell no one, are ya? Y'ain't gonna turn me in?"

"Turn you in? Who'd want you? Don't even know a creek from a river! Don't you got no schools down there? You just spend all your time saying 'y'all' and chasing black people away from the drinking fountain?" He pitched another rock. "Strike three!"

In town, I hiked to The Brown Ungulate for an invigorating platter of starch and animal fat. A lot of the food up here is the sort you stare at for a long time. I was served by a very small woman who could barely see over the table top. At the table next to me, three very large women laughed about the musclemen they had flirted with in the fitness club. It was a study in contrasts.

Back on Main Street, I bought a few cans of food, a box of raisin bran, and a carton of milk for my backpack. Then, on a whim, I picked up a baseball in Homer's Ace Hardware. Back

Billy in the Shade

on the sidewalk, I glanced in Gopher's Barber Shop, where men lounged here and there dishing the poop. I waved, but I don't think they saw me.

The day had warmed under a clear sky, and I walked back to the bridge and then into the countryside along the county road. The sun was behind me, so my shadow led the way. Occasionally, a driveway twisted away among trees and their shadows to the houses of other hermits and refugees. There was a Carlson sign on one of the mailboxes, and I wondered if it was Bob of the shellacked walleye and split personality.

Later that evening I sat on the stoop by my door as my little oval of evening sky started to do its old connect-the-dots thing. The starlight here is brighter than I ever saw in New Orleans, where it is all bleached out from the city. I thought about how we don't actually see the stars but just the light that left them anywhere from hundreds to billions of years ago. And a shiver swirled through me on the stoop as I thought about how the star I see may have exploded thousands of years ago. We only see the memory of a star.

• • •

By the way, God, You're kind of quiet. Once You said that in the beginning was the word. Why don't we get any words from You now? You might like to know that a couple of years ago Kyle, the guy I hung with in New Orleans, got a personalized response to his letter to the President about the war.

The response was mainly just to correct Kyle's grammar and stuff. It said that "shithead" is still two words (I don't think so), and also that the President's rectum is not pink and does not have a beach umbrella inserted in it. But it *was* a response. Not that I think the President and his staff are busier than You and

After the Floods

the angels. But I would like to hear from You. Maybe You could also tell me what happened to Kyle, who disappeared in the hurricane. Oh well.

Suggestion: You might want to clean up the interstellar debris. Like Mom always said, appearances matter! And You'll feel better, too. It's win-win.

Problem: If Jesus was resurrected bodily and traveled at the speed of light, he'd still be in this galaxy. And why would he need a body in heaven anyway? Please get back to me.

Billy Talks to Sister Ann

To: Sister Ann
From: Billy B.
CC: God
Re: Advice

Dear Sister Ann:

Yo. I know it's only been two or three weeks since I found your website and signed up for advice with my credit card. You're probably busy just like God (only different). But it's spring and I need to get started making a new life. Sometimes I go outside at night to look at the stars, which are way beautiful but also confusing.

Like I said, I live in the woods near a town. I came here last fall and had never seen (or felt!) winter before. Sometimes the electricity was out and I couldn't even charge my cell phone, but who would I call anyway? And then there was that sound at night like someone tapping. Freaked? C'est moi. I guess it was just ice cracking.

I feel better now and want to meet nice people and be liked, and I thought that you could help. I thought that you could tell me what the tricks are for being liked. I don't want to go insane like Kyle, a guy I hung with until it got too weird. So my question is, how do we not be lonely? I'm sure you know all the secrets, and I have paid $75 for three months of advice.

I hope you are well,
Billy B.

P.S. Like I said in my first email, I'm twenty-four. The other day I met a boy throwing stones into the creek who is about ten. We joked around a little. Is that okay? I'm not a peddlefile (sp?).

He Delivers a Pitch

To: God
From: Billy B.
CC: Sister Ann
Subject: Happy things, spooky things

Since buying the baseball, the summer days have started to skid by. I've read *War and Peace*. Okay, I skipped parts. I skipped everything about Pierre, who was dull as dough. Probably that was Tolstoy's purpose, but why? Just for variety? I guess You tossed some nuts into Your salad, too. Glenn Beck? Billy Boichild?

Besides reading, I've also tried to figure a cool way to pass the baseball on to the kid. Before buying the ball, I saw him in the yard of a small, white house along the county road. He was with a spiffy woman in jeans who's got to be his mom. Yesterday I walked to town along the road, but the yard, full

After the Floods

of crocuses, a maple tree, assorted shrubs, and some birds, was empty of humans.

This morning I had planned to walk the creek, but at the last minute I decided to trick fate and take the road again. Yesss! It worked! Fate is as dumb as a box of rocks. The kid was sitting in the yard next to a chocolate lab curled up like a sausage on its shadow. The boy gazed at a crow in the grass a few feet away, and the crow seemed to look back at him, cocking its head quizzically. I figured I'd just flip the ball into the yard and keep walking without looking the boy's way. Cool. I'd be the ultra mysterious baseball-flipper guy.

"Hey mister!" the kid shouted. In a moment I heard his sneakers padding behind me. "Mister, wait up!"

I stopped and turned as he slowed to a walk, tossing the ball in the air and catching it with a snap that reminded me of how my dad used to toss apples in the air. The kid wore a Twins cap over light brown hair.

"This ball just landed in my yard," he said. "You know anything about that?"

"Confuzzles me," I said. "I was in this car accident, and it knocked the sense right out of me. I heard it hails golf balls up here, but I didn't know baseballs drop out of the sky."

"Confuzzles? Is that confusion with fuzz on top?"

"It's more to do with being puzzled," I said, "but I like how your mind works."

We stepped further from the road as a car from the dark ages crept by, halting and flatulent.

"Well, that stuff about hail and golf balls is just what you call a figure of speech. Like metaphors. Ain't you learning anything up here, for crying out loud?"

"I didn't hear you," I replied. "I was listening to the chickadees

Billy in the Shade

over in the poplars, or maybe they're in that jack pine over there. But what does crine . . . ?"

"Get out!" he exclaimed, doing a big jaw-drop thing. "You should go on Stupid Pet Tricks, you're getting so smart!"

"Your mom let you stay up to watch David Letterman? Kinda late for a ten year old, isn't it?"

"Eleven," he replied. "I only get to stay up late when I'm with Uncle Mike. Mom always has me take a nap the next day. We call it a napule, which is a little nap with Mudface. But I'm not supposed to talk to strangers, and you're strange, in case you didn't know."

His cap was off now, and his hair, to which the sunlight added a layer of fur, moved in the breeze.

"How do you get Gopher to leave all that hair on your head?" I asked. "He likes it short as a putting green."

"Mom cuts my hair," he replied. "I wouldn't let that quack near my head."

"A quack barber?"

"Isn't that what we say?"

"Only if he does duck tails."

"I don't get it."

"Duck tails? Like on Elvis Presley? Never mind."

"You scared the crow away," he announced. "I was learning all about New Orleans."

That was weird, since I didn't remember telling him I was from The Big Easy. Before I could respond he turned away, shaking his head in mock disgust, and walked back toward his house. I had forgotten to clarify the "crine out loud" issue. As I started off toward town, he yelled, "Thanks, mister!" I waved without turning, the way-cool backwards wave.

Then I remembered what Gopher had said about Sower hair-

After the Floods

cuts. Could the kid and his mom be members of that mysterious group? Did they have boiling cauldrons in the cellar, one with the Boichild label taped to its side?

Coming home from town later in the day, I decided to wander a while out by the creek. It was way too fresh and warm to sit around in my trailer. I came to a fence where wild flowers decorated the grass with purple, yellow, and red spangles, and I wondered about their names. Beyond the fence stretched a stubble field where two men attacked the earth with shovels. Three women looked on, wearing ancient skirts and scarves that wrapped about their heads like bandages. Stones were piled here and there, and some sticks jutted from the ground.

Suddenly one of the women pointed at me. The men stuck their spades in the dirt and slowly turned, and at that moment I realized, with a chill scampering down my back, that it was a do-it-yourself cemetery. They all stood still as ice and stared, and then one of the men pulled a cell phone from his pocket and thumbed it. Certain that I'd been telesnorted into Stephen King's brain, I tried to fade back into the shadows of the birch and poplar without looking absolutely, wack-job freaked.

It was a troubled night, filled with spooky sounds in the trees. It was July 4th, and fireworks were going off over by the river. In my patch of open sky, the moon through the mist was silver like a DVD fresh out of the box—*Night of the Living Dead*, probably.

• • •

Hey, really, Most Intelligent of Designers Guy. I know You're busy. You've probably been getting after that interstellar debris. That's great, but I could use some intelligent advice. I gotta decide what to do with myself, and I'm not buying the barber's notion that killing fish will help.

120

Billy in the Shade

My money's running short, and I hate to keep spare-changing Dad. He already pays my credit card bills. I bet You know what I mean, like: "Dear God on High, gimme this, gimme that." But I'm not asking You for a handout, just some all-wise, all-knowing (and all free) advice. No one asked You to be God. It was Your idea. You woke up one morning and decided to be God, and God has a lot of jobs. So put down that broom and start talking. The rest of the space debris can wait.

I didn't mean to be bossy. Tell You what, I'm gonna go to that park in town tomorrow, the one down the block from the hardware store, and sit on the bench. Then I'll pick up the first scrap of paper that blows by. Just a few words will be fine. If paper doesn't work, tex-mess me on my celly. Don't worry about the spelling.

Tootles.

P.S. Did You decide to be God, or were You born God? How did all that work? Youth wants to know.

A Cop Checks Him Out

To: God
From: William Boichild
CC: The Void
Subject: Life (mine) on Earth

Yesterday I parked the Civic around the corner from Cold Beak's main street, called Main Street. There's a drug store on the corner with lettering on the window announcing, I swear, Moody Drugs.

After the Floods

If you duck in (not You, just anyone—You can see through walls, right?), you find a dim place cluttered with Ludens Cherry-Flavored Cough Drops, Ace Bandages, Bayer Aspirin, and a few hundred other resources for the self-medicater. Behind a walled-off inner sanctum, Moody himself glides about in a white jacket, noiselessly shaking, stirring, and counting.

Moody is spooky. Occasionally someone slouches to a window, shoves a piece of paper Moody's way, and after ten minutes receives a mysterious product designated by a trained professional in the disease business, a product such as Lexapro or Viagra named after a supernatural being in a comic book. In the dim light that Moody prefers, it all seems sort of film noir.

Next door to Moody's, and by way of contrast, is Lund's Grocery, a bright vacation land of juices and cereals, Cokes and ice cream. Then comes Homer's Ace Hardware, the three stores forming a progression from illness to health to industriousness.

Homer's Ace is Cold Beak's one hardware store, and I rummaged around in there yesterday with some home improvement in mind. I checked out hammers, lifting them to gauge their weight and feel, like Tiger Woods selecting a driver. Suddenly a very macro dude in a sheriff's uniform lumbered up and extended a hand big as a catcher's mitt.

"I'm Mike Maki," he said. "I've been meaning to introduce myself for a few days now."

Mike did not look like someone you'd want to mess with, but his manner was friendly and his handshake, reminding me of Coach's (my old high school football coach), did only minimal cartilage damage.

"Listen," Mike said, "I'm on a little break here, and I thought I'd park my carcass on the bench down in the town square. Why

Billy in the Shade

don't you stop out there when you find the nails to go with that hammer? We could talk a little."

I told him I had planned to stop there in any case, although I didn't mention the message that I hoped You would send.

The town square has a fountain, a pastel assembly of stuff for kids to climb, and a statue of a local ancestor gazing heroically at the aluminum roof of Dick Moody's enterprise, or perhaps down the side street where I had parked. It was a rockin' summer day, and a little bench time would be diggity. The bench, which was in the shade of a tree (I haven't learned what kind yet), was flocked with bird droppings. They looked like they were dry, though, and I sat down next to Mike, tossing the brown paper bag from Homer's by my feet. Behind us, two kids argued as they slapped a tether ball back and forth.

"Nice day," Mike observed, reaching in his pocket and producing something in a red and green wrapper. "Nut Goodie? I used to chew snoose, but now I'm all Nut Goodies. They're made in Minnesota. Chocolate and nuts."

"My face would look like a pepperoni pizza," I said. "Sorry."

"Too bad. I find a Nut Goodie puts folks at ease."

"I'm good," I assured him.

A pregnant woman passed in front of us with two children in tow, the three of them loudly debating ice cream flavors.

"Marva Updahl," Mike said, shaking his head, "fertile as Iowa. Six kids going on seven, and she ain't even Catholic. No offense."

"None taken," I assured him.

"Always talking," Mike said, still shaking his head, "with more lose screws than a junkyard. When she don't have any kids with her she talks to God, right out here on the street. Folks worry about how that herd of hers will turn out."

After the Floods

"Folks overhear any responses?" I asked.

"From God?"

"Well, yeah."

Mike laughed. "No, I suppose it's like when you hear someone on a cell phone. All you catch is the one side." Then he switched the topic to me. "So," he began, "I hear they call you Alligator."

I noticed the close shave above his ears. "I think you've been over to Gopher's Hair and News Service. Alligator is his invention."

"Yeah, I bet from the dawn of grooming the barber shop has been a hub of local info-tainment," he declared, smiling. "It's good to know some things don't change, don't you think?"

"Maybe, although I get the impression that if Gopher knows it, everyone knows it."

"There is that. But listen, I hear that little Sandy Elden has been giving you vocabulary lessons," Mike said after disappearing a chunk of candy into his disturbingly large mouth. "He tell you what snoose is? Snoose is what folks from elsewhere call snuff."

It was the first time that I'd heard the boy's name, but I told Mike that I had picked up on snoose without Sandy's instructions. You hear about snoose pretty fast when you get to Minnesota. Gopher even had a couple of old but functioning spittoons in his shop; I remember, because the guys' accuracy had been off that day and Gopher had muttered about getting bathtubs.

"Well, it's like this," Mike said. "I'm gonna be absolutely straight ahead with you. Siiri, that's Sandy's mother, Siiri is my kid sister, which makes Sandy my nephew last time I checked. Now when you hear that a stranger has been talking to your nephew out in the woods and giving him a baseball . . . well, it makes you decide to introduce yourself. There's no offense intended. I'm not saying anything is wrong here. You understand?"

Billy in the Shade

In my smart-ass college days I might have been offended, but now I wasn't. "You gotta take care of the kids," I said. I flashed on what Grandpa wrote in *The Chronicles* about how some of the Boichilds lurking in the family tree were known as Boinkchilds. I stayed cool, though, since I'd long-ago convinced myself that boinking children wasn't genetic. I even congratulated myself on my maturity, although Mike's size had a lot to do with my co-operative attitude.

"You're doing the right thing," I assured him.

"Good," he said. "I'm real glad to know that, because here's the deal. Folks around here believe in hospitality, like they do down in Atlanta, where you come from. My friends in the God Squad tell me that welcoming the stranger happens all over the place in the Bible. I wouldn't know, but I know that hospitality is one of those things that separate civilized people from the thugs and terrorists. And we want to welcome you."

I told him I appreciated that.

"The deal is, though," he went on, "you got us at a disadvantage. You can see who we are right out in the open. Our jobs, our property, our relatives and friendships—all that stuff is pretty visible to anyone with eyes that focus. But you're the Invisible Man. No one knows anything about you. Your family? Don't know. Your education? Don't know. Net worth? Big mystery. You see where I'm going with this?"

This time I said that I wasn't sure.

"What I'm saying is, it's real nice of you to stop and chat with a kid by the creek and a few days later give him a baseball. But let us know who you are. Now I'm guessing you must have some cash somewhere. Walk on over to Pioneer National and open a checking account. In the process they'll write down your social security number."

125

After the Floods

Mike paused to jam in more chocolate and nuts.

"And that Mobile station on the edge of town?" he continued after some heavy chewing. "Byron was telling me the other day that he could use a part-time guy. Those fused fingers of his give him trouble. And get yourself a Minnesota driver's license. You're driving illegal right now. What I'm saying is, join the community."

Macro Mike interrupted himself again, this time to gaze at a man with a face like a scribble who hobbled by Moody's in a rumpled suit and sneakers. He was followed out of the drugstore by a thirty-something woman in cool jeans.

"That's Lars Johnson," Macro observed. "Used to be mayor of Cold Beak. Got his face discombobulated in Vietnam. He says he's writing a history of the town. That other one's Mattie. She runs the kitchen out at The Phoenix."

"Nice hair," I said.

"Which one?"

"The old guy."

"Yeah, like a pile of lint."

For a moment Mike seemed to have stalled somewhere back down memory lane with Lars, or maybe Mattie, then he got the engine running and returned to the issue of the strange Boichild.

"You probably don't know how long you're gonna stay here in Cold Beak," he went on, "and that's not the point. The point is, give us someone with defining features, someone to know. You do that, and people will be inviting you over for bratwursts and a Twins game on TV faster than you can learn the name of another bird by the creek. Now that's the end of my speech, and I hope you ain't offended."

I told him that I understood and appreciated everything he had said, and I meant it. I had grown up with a firewall protecting my

126

Billy in the Shade

alleged brain from the virus of common-sense, but he'd managed to sneak some of his through to me. So I went on to say that I had graduated from Loyola University in New Orleans and that my father had been a furniture dealer. His website was still up, and Mike could check it out.

I didn't mention my religious work in the Big Sleazy. It isn't that I was ashamed about my ex-religion, but I hadn't sorted out my feelings about the research hospital. We had wanted to build a hospital to explore ways to implant faith through surgery, drugs, and electromagnetism. And there was the spiritual detective agency. Once Kyle and I had accepted cash to hunt for some poor slob's lost faith, a job that required us to spend many nights in French Quarter bars. It turned out the guy had meant a lost *dog* named Faith. That was before Kyle got weird.

Okay. I *was* ashamed. Sometimes I hate it how You know everything. It better be true that You *do* know everything! I don't want to die and find out it was just a crowd-control story.

"You're not from Atlanta then?" Mike asked.

"No," I said, "but Gopher was watching *Gone With the Wind* with Little Mouse, and . . . It's a long story."

Mike laughed. "Well, Gopher himself is a long story. Started a big controversy last year when he let Bob Carlson pay for a haircut with a couple of walleye fillets. Next few days, Carlson was up and down Main Street trying to buy things with walleyes. He kept insisting on paying for his oil change in fish, for crying out loud. Kept calling law enforcement to ask about the laws.

"Local businessmen had to call a meeting," Maki continued, "and in a week or two *The Peep* ran an article on how you couldn't pay with fillets in Cold Beak. *The Peep* spelled it all out. How a business couldn't very well pay its income tax by sending in hunks of walleye, how there'd be storage issues and shipping

After the Floods

issues, not to mention odor issues. And anyway, when we get the federal assistance for schools, we don't want to get hunks of old fish. You don't want to start a fish-in/fish-out type of thing with Washington."

"I guess that settled it," I said.

"Not for Bob. He wrote a rebuttal in that little notebook of his and then included a chart showing how many ounces of walleye ought to equal a gallon of gas. It's framed on the wall over at Moose's, right by the Fool of the Week Board. Why, one afternoon at Moose's, Carlson got to inventing an exchange rate, since people might want to pay with other kinds of fish."

"Like dollars, euros, and yen?" I asked.

"Exactly. Carlson used the walleye standard, and charted out on a napkin how many ounces of bass or northern pike would equal one ounce of walleye. Next thing you know he was talkin' about lending and borrowing at the Pioneer National Walleye Bank. When old Lester Olson ridiculed the idea, Carlson got mean and I had to slap the cuffs on him. He'd only had five beers. That was in *The Peep* too. Now he calls me all the time about whether some new scheme of his will land him in jail."

"Some people have weird ways of sticking themselves in the world," I said.

"That's for sure. It ain't easy broadcasting reality through to Bob Carlson. He's got like a busted antenna, you might say. You probably saw some of that in New Orleans. Me and Carlson, we get along okay, though, thanks to caller I.D." Maki paused a moment, as an orchestra of robins landed in the branches above us. "We better get out from under this tree," he suggested. "I got splattered pretty good the other day talking reality to one of our troubled teens under a tree."

128

Billy in the Shade

We stood up, stepped away, and shook hands just as a Popsicle wrapper fluttered down from the sky. I grabbed the wrapper and saw that someone (You?) had written "Yo" on the back. Overhead, two crows gazed down from a power line. A larger family of them squatted like smudges atop Moody Drugs, and the robins tuned their instruments in the tree.

"What's that?" Maki asked, giving me the questioning eyebrows. "You collect Popsicle wrappers?"

"Well," I replied after examining the wrapper, "it isn't a message from God."

"Okay," he said, smiling, "this has been great. We're getting to know each other."

"I'm glad," I said, allowing him to wrap his hand around mine and shake it like an animal with its prey.

"I gotta go catch a few folks reinterpreting the speed laws out on Highway 2. Gotta make my quota. If you shoot pool, I'm usually in Moose's Pit Stop from five to six. I got a two-beer limit, though. Guys at the barber shop are gonna tell you soon enough how I was before they dragged me into AA. That was after my divorce," he dropped my hand and looked up at the birds hopping about in the tree.

"I got a daughter who lives in Des Moines now," he continued. "She calls at Christmas to remind me of my sins. Seems like the list is still growing. But it's true I always had a six pack in my brain. Got my name on Moose's Fool Board plenty of times." He laughed in a tentative, forced sort of way. "I gotta laugh about it now," he explained. "It's part of the cure. Later, Alligator."

He paused to say hello to two dwarfs passing on the sidewalk, and then he jay-walked to his copmobile. It was odd that he had told me about the divorce and the hostile daughter, odd and

After the Floods

generous, as though he was showing me what it is to let another person know you.

I watched the dwarfs trundle off in the afternoon sun. Their oversized butts were like duffel bags, and their shadows were little blankets dangling out. That's when I realized that Cold Beak is over-dwarfed, like maybe a colony settled here.

• • •

Thanks for the Popsicle wrapper, Dude. You give good swag. But why did You invent dwarfs? What's the point of gimpification? Could You get back to me on that? The cripples here are almost as sad as the crosstitutes in New Orleans. Are there gimps where You are, like with fused wings maybe? Any crosstitute angels in drag? Or did You rig it so only us folks down here get those way cool features? Just curious. I'm not judging here. I'm not a Seventh Day Judgmentalist.

But Dude, You keep everything so mysterious. You're just flashing us the public side, the scrubbed and polished side. What do You do in Your time off, in Your chillin' time? You got a favorite star? You drink Bud or Miller? What do You and Your Son dish about in the evening? Did He have hard feelings about getting nailed up? Does life, like, go on for You? Does Jesus still live at home?

You need to show us the human side, Man. Like Big Mike said, we want to welcome the stranger, but You gotta meet us half way. The trouble with You is, there's no one there to know. You gotta dehermitize, just like me.

• • •

When I said to Mike that we have to take care of the children, I realized that sometimes children have to take care of their par-

Billy in the Shade

ents. I was thinking about Dad, who's by himself now in New Orleans. Maybe I should be helping him. Don't worry, I don't expect an answer.

Later, Stranger

A Meeting by the Well

To: Sister Ann
From: Billy B.
CC:
Subject: A babe in the woods

Hi Sis. I need to tell you about how I met Siiri.
When weather allows, I hike to town to help out at Byron's filling station. Byron rents me the trailer cheap, so I'm glad to do it. A new restaurant opened near his station. It's called The Phonics, or something like that. Anyway, he's been busy. It's spooky how new buildings are popping up everywhere. There's a glass and steel bank on the edge of town where, I swear, the lot was vacant two days ago. Should I see a doctor?

But I was talking about Byron. He's got fingers that came out of the womb stuck together, and it makes it hard to handle tools. It's like he's got swim fins on his hands, and now arthritis is adding to the drama. So he sits back and offers suggestions. He's the mind and I'm the body, like in Descartes or Rex Stout. It reminds me of the times I helped Dad in the furniture store on Canal Street, except that I was the brains in Dad's store. Oh I know, he only let me pretend I was the brains. Anyway, Byron taught me to fix tires, do an oil change, and change a windshield wiper. I'm a trained professional.

After the Floods

Byron likes to talk about deer hunting, which he took up a few years ago, learning to pull the trigger with his third finger. But last fall he was hobbled and couldn't go. I'm not into killing animals, but I keep it to myself. Everyone hunts around here. Byron likes to talk about his hunting days, and I like to hear him talk.

On my way home from work last Tuesday I managed to meet Siiri Elden, Sheriff Mike Maki's sister. In spiffy jeans (no mom jeans for her) and a plaid shirt, she was pumping water from a well in her yard. The well is in the shade of a maple tree, and it was a banging scene perfect for a postcard. Sandy's chocolate lab was busy training him to throw a stick, as crows made a row of cheerleaders on the power line.

"There he is," Sandy called to his mother. "There's that Confederate who came here to be a hermit and learn about birds and trees."

Clearly, I had been discussed. Pros and cons had been weighed. Maybe a vote had been taken, or the issue tabled pending more information. I waved. As Sandy waved back, his mother put her bucket down, brushed back a lock of hair, and floated toward me. I'm sure she floated, because I checked for wires like a kid at a magic show. Then all three of them approached at their different speeds, Sandy warning Mudface, the loping dog, not to run out on the road. The yard was bounded by a white wooden fence, which Sandy straddled. I said hi.

"So, you're the mysterious stranger that makes baseballs drop from the sky," Siiri said, again brushing a cloud of light brown hair from her eyes. "Why don't you come into the yard and have a glass of lemonade? I'm Siiri."

She offered a hand, pushing it forward in a prompt, down-home, country sort of way that modified the image of the

Billy in the Shade

ethereal floater from Fantasy Land. I managed to rest her hand in my own, the way you might handle a rare orchid.

"Mom makes awesome lemonade," Sandy assured me. His Twins cap was absent, and his hair was nearly blond in the summer sun.

"My name is Bill, and I drink awesome lemonade every chance I get. Thanks," I replied, walking around to the driveway and knowing that I'd already said something really stupid—*I drink awesome lemonade every chance I get*. I need a dumbectomy.

"Uncle Mike says your last name is Boichild," Sandy offered. "You could change that, couldn't you? I mean now that you're older?" He ducked his mother's mock dope-slap.

"Never," I said sternly. "I'm the last of a long line. A Boichild was dubbed First Among His Majesty's Fops under Charles II. The Boichilds juggled skulls for George III. It's a noble heritage. There's even a leather-bound book all about us."

"I'd lose it," Sandy insisted. "Sit, Mudface!"

"It's a good book, a family treasure."

"I meant the name. Duh!"

"Try to be polite, Sandy," his mom said, "just while I get the lemonade. I know it's hard."

Siiri is slim, with a nice bounce in her step, and I watched a little too long as she walked toward the house to keep the beverage promise. A row of impatiens lined the brick walkway.

"You aren't supposed to stare at her butt," Sandy informed me as he stooped to pick up a Frisbee. "Up here in civilization it isn't polite. We learned about it in school. I took Civility."

"Oops," I admitted.

"Mudface can catch a Frisbee in the air," he said. "Watch!"

He flipped it sidearm, and the blue disk floated, a ghostly UFO, out across the yard, turning slowly toward the picket

After the Floods

fence where a bicycle lay on its side in the grass, its handlebars and front wheel jutting upward at an angle. Mudface loped along beneath the Frisbee, leapt, cork-screwed in the air, and came down with the prey.

"Groovisimo!" Sandy shouted. "Bring it here now!"

"Good boy," I added, getting in the spirit of things.

"Mudface is a girl," Sandy informed me. "She'll lie on her back and show you."

"I'll take it on faith," I replied. "She *is* sweetness dogified."

"Dogified," Sandy repeated with a giggle.

He flipped the Frisbee my way, and it skidded to my feet. "Oops! Gravity test!" he proclaimed. Then it was my turn to shake off the doggy drool and fling it. I made the team in no time.

Siiri returned along the impatiens path with a pitcher of lemonade and glasses on a tray, and we sat in the shade at a picnic table by the pump. Two squirrels barber-poled down the maple, exploding out of the shade and into a zig-zagging chase across the sun-warmed lawn. As Siiri poured for each of us, a large pink bubble blossomed from her lips and burst.

"You can do bigger ones than that, Mom," Sandy insisted. Then he told me that his mother had been the bubble-gum champion of the sixth grade.

"That was a long time ago, Sandy. I'm kinda off my game now."

"Just think if she'd saved all the baseball cards!" Sandy exclaimed. "We'd be rich! I keep telling her."

Siiri kissed his head and laughed, and her laughter reminded me of a river bubbling and rolling. I learned, as gum snapped and the Frisbee flew, that Siiri is a nurse in the small, regional hospital on the other side of Cold Beak. She's been working overtime, and I asked if there was an epidemic in the area.

"Well, you might call it that I suppose," she said guardedly.

134

Billy in the Shade

"Actually, it's a problem we've had for a decade now, since the Sowers moved in. They don't take good care of themselves . . . or their kids." Siiri inserted her wad of gum back in its wrapper.

Gopher had mentioned the Sowers on the day he learned to use the scissors. I think they are a religious group, always talked about in a cryptic, say-no-more way. Sandy seemed about to let a few cats wiggle out of the bag, but Siiri's glance tightened the drawstring and he took a sudden interest in the grove of poplar trees beyond the fence. Then I noticed a tear in Siiri's eye, and she saw me notice.

"I was thinking about Gerald Lund," she explained. "He's the young man who died in Iraq, leaving his son without a father. You probably heard about the funeral. I guess we don't take good care of our kids either."

"Yes," I said, "Byron talked about it at the gas station. I'm sorry."

Eventually, Siiri plucked a blade of grass, examined it, and put it between her teeth. For the next couple of minutes it was talk about the weather. Did I hear that streets had flooded in New Orleans? I informed Siiri that pumps always fail and streets always flood in New Orleans. There is aquatic life that lives dormant in the potholes from one flood to the next, and litter migrates about the city by water.

"I suppose they'll get that fixed," Siiri remarked.

"Yeah," Sandy scoffed, "when puppies don't poop. Those people don't know a creek from a river."

"Who told you that?" I asked defensively.

"That crow you scared away with the baseball."

"You should come to dinner tonight," Siiri suggested, after zapping Sandy with an exaggerated frown. "It's just hot dish, but I'm having my brother over. He tells me the two of you are becoming old buds."

After the Floods

"Uncle Mike will be glad to know that you were staring at Mom's butt just now," Sandy ventured. "He was worried you might be one of those guys that likes little boys."

"Well," Siiri said with a sigh, "what a relief to have the orientation issue cleared up." She did her bubbling-river laugh again, her New Hope laugh. "Why don't you stop back in about an hour?"

The world keeps morphing into a weird planet with an atmosphere that I can't breathe. Or sometimes it's like I've been shoved into a strange stage play and I don't know my lines. Anyway, I spent the hour alone feeling like a twitchy kid prepping for his first date, worrying about the cologne issue and the clothing issue. It was deja childhood. Would I find things to say, or would I be reduced to phonemes while grinning like a jack-o-lantern? What if I got the nether vapors at the dinner table, or got one of those four-hour erections you hear so much about on TV?

These worries followed me like a pack of ghouls out to the fence by the Sowers' cemetery (?), where I picked a colorful bunch of wild flowers, hoping that Sandy wouldn't quiz me on their names. There was no one in the cemetery, and the sticks-and-stones monuments were crumbly and pathetic. A mockingbird took flight from a tree above me, which was a surprise. Mockingbirds are supposed to be reserved for the South. But like I said, Cold Beak has birds from everywhere. It must be a pilgrimage thing.

Anyway, I put together an armful of flowers that looked good to my eye, and I sauntered back to the trailer to clean up.

Billy in the Shade

Billy Dines Out

To: Sister Ann
From: Billy
CC:
Subject: Love

When Siiri met me at her door with violet lipstick and the scent of jasmine, I went all out of tune, my hands shaking, my pits sweating . . . there was a flood inside me. She was half Siiri and half my first high-school girlfriend stirred together in a dream jumble, and her face was like that place in the trees where the sun comes through. I jerked the flowers up and held them between us, where they trembled for a century or two as I squeezed the stalks like a drowning doofus clutching straws. My mouth opened and closed without releasing words, and all the while my eyes swarmed over her face that peeked at me from around the bouquet. Then she smiled thanks through one of those mists of hair that women produce just to render you totally, bangingly, and forever at their mercy.

Macro Mike arrived around six-thirty, raising ghostly puffs of dust in the driveway with his copmobile. A new fat farm had been built on a hill by the town, and Mike complained about the traffic problems. But he'd managed to spend his usual hour after work whacking pool balls at Moose's. Siiri showed me where to sit, and the "hot dish" was served, which turns out to be Minnesota talk for a casserole made up of whatever the hands of yesterday stashed in the fridge.

I had survived the pantomime of the posies. As we ate, my brain cells regrouped and swam back into familiar waters. By the

After the Floods

time Sandy started campaigning for dessert, I congratulated my-self on having said more than *yeah* and *okay* while emitting no socially unacceptable Billy fumes. Sandy had flipped on the TV.

"Mom! That's the ad I was asking about, the one about a reptile dysfunction. I don't get it."

A cell phone played a tune, giving Siiri a reason to ignore Sandy's question and leaving him shaking his head.

"It's the hospital," Siiri reported, snapping her phone shut. "I gotta go."

"Well sport," Mike said to Sandy, "looks to me like you get to go to jail again."

"Warp-cool!" Sandy exclaimed. "Can I mess with the hand-cuffs and torture stuff again?"

"Sandy," Siiri scolded, "you'll give Bill the wrong impression. He'll think it's just like New Orleans here."

It didn't seem like the right moment to protest.

Sandy would spend the night with his uncle, and Siiri would get in touch with them on her cell as soon as the situation at the hospital was clear. So the party ended early. The looks that Mike and Siiri traded made it clear that there were things I didn't know, but it wasn't a time for questions. Since it was still light outside, I said I'd walk back to my trailer in the woods, but Mike insisted on driving.

Although it was bingo night, the parking lot by the church on the county road was empty. After leaving the county road, we bounced along the gravel to my trailer. I made a mental note to find out why gravel roads buckle into giant rib cages in Minnesota, and then I told Macro about the cemetery I'd stumbled across with the dour diggers and their women in skirts from the dark ages.

"They were probably just burying a dog," I concluded. "But it was weird the way they stopped to stare at me."

Billy in the Shade

"That would be the Sowers," he said. "And no, it probably wasn't just a dog. They think they commune with dragons or something. There's some stuff going on around here, and I'm not comfortable with you out here by yourself."

"People are so fake," Sandy put in, "pretending it's religion when it's just being mean."

"I don't understand," I said. Then I mentioned how, when they saw me, they had gone for their cell phones.

"They were probably trying to phone God," Sandy said. "That's how crazy they are."

"Maybe we can talk tomorrow," Mike suggested. "Stop by the office if you're in town."

"If you're still alive," Sandy added cheerfully.

The car ground to a stop in the gravel by my shack. A doe and her two offspring bounded from my sad excuse for a yard, flashing the white bottoms of their tails against the deepening darkness in the underbrush and trees. I waved goodbye as I climbed out of the car, repressing a "tootles" that almost slipped by the censor like an agent of the past. Kyle and I had said "tootles" in New Orleans.

Despite the spookiness of Macro's goodbye, I spent the next hour or two *chez moi* alternately grinning at the walls of the doublewide and sitting outside to look at the stars, all because of Siiri, with her bubble gum and good cheer. The threads in destiny's fabric diverge and converge in an endless weave. I had lost my New Orleans friends, but now there was Siiri, not to mention her two guys. She had baked a hot dish of desire in my oven, a hot dish of left-over hopes all stirred up and seasoned with something bangingly new and delicious.

There were northern lights that night, swelling up over the trees and flowing across the sky like green and blue flames. They

After the Floods

were how I felt inside. It was more of that fractal thing, the inner world and the outer world being the same only different. Maybe I'm just wired to think that everything is also something else.

It was strange, though, how right in the middle of the happy thoughts about Siiri, sad thoughts came like muffled thunder beyond hills. They were mostly thoughts about how Mom died and how Dad is getting old. Happiness never comes alone. It always drags a shadow.

Am I crazy? I need an opinion.

• • •

Sister Ann, when I first signed up for your advice I was worried about meeting people. Now I've met Siiri, and I really don't want to blow it. So now I really need to know all the secrets that people with good relationships know. I want to be a good guy for her, and I don't want to make her like me just with tricks and cool lines. I want it to be really me, and you're my online guardian angel.

Please tell me how I can be really me and at the same time get Siiri to like me, which could be incompatible events. She's only two or three years older than I am (I think). Is it already a strike against me that I got caught looking at her butt?

Handcuffs and Lemonade

To: God
From: William Boichild
CC: The Attorney General
Subject: Rotten people!!

Billy in the Shade

I filled the kitchen sink, spread a towel on the floor, and scrubbed my naked self with Joy on a sponge. Then I climbed into my dress blue jeans, selected from Target's elegant collection, and drove into town to see Macro Mike Maki. It was the day after Siiri's hot dish and Macro's spooky goodbye, and I was as happy as springtime wrapped in clean skin. As my Civic approached the water tower, two helicopters swooped and hovered like hawks over the far side of town. State Troopers were parked outside of Mike's office, and a stranger in uniform lounged at the doorway.

"Hi there," I said. "I'm a friend of Mike Maki. He asked me to stop by today. Is he around?"

"Hey! That's my friend Bill," Sandy shouted, poking his head out of the door. "He's from the South and we're trying to educate him. Bill's in love with Mom, but he's too young. She married a young guy last time. Mom's twenty-nine."

"The sheriff and his deputy are taking care of a disturbance at the hospital, and I'm holding down the fort here," the man in uniform said. "But if you're a friend of the family, you could go in and talk to Sandy for a while." His lips added a silent *please*. "I gotta stay outside and keep the riff-raff away."

"It's those Sowers," Sandy said, swinging on the door. "They brought guns and everything! Uncle Mike had to call State Troopers from all around the county. I heard him on the radio when it was still dark this morning! Wanna try on my handcuffs?"

We walked into Mike's office, and I told Sandy that I'd rather hear more about the Sowers.

"I could lock you in a cell. I know how! You could beg for food, and then I could tell you all about them."

"Why don't you sit behind the desk, put your feet up like a fat old cop in a movie, and give me the poop on what's happening."

141

After the Floods

"Sure," Sandy said, taking his position behind the desk, hoisting his feet, and planting his heels on his book of sudoku puzzles. "Ain't I supposed to have a box of donuts?"

"It's an imperfect world, Sandy."

He gave a colorful version of Sower history. They had bought eighty acres outside of Cold Beak a decade ago, having traveled eastward from Arizona in old minivans decorated with biblical passages. They had been in a fundamentalist sect out there, but they got tired of whatever lunatic was directing the show. Besides, they had their own lunatic.

"All the men have a bunch of wives, but there's one guy who tells everyone who to marry. He's called Saint Bob. Sometimes you have to marry your sister! Sometimes your sister is your mother! It's warp-weird."

"Aren't there laws about that in Minnesota? Why hasn't Uncle Mike tossed them in jail?"

"That's what Mom says, but he says it's hard to prove things because they're all brainwashed. The women are too scared too tell and don't know how to live on their own anyway." Sandy was fiddling with a pair of handcuffs as he talked. "Mike thinks they drove a 4x4 full of guns and stuff over to a group in North Dakota last winter. He also says they're baked on drugs all the time."

"Nothing says Christmas like an assault rifle."

"Yeah," Sandy said, "imagine the elves adjusting them on the target range."

"You're a visual dude. But what does it all have to do with the hospital?"

"Mom says the men don't allow women or children to go to the hospital, but sometimes a woman takes a sick baby there anyway. Last year Saint Bob warned the doctors and nurses not to take care of any of the women and children. So this time they

Billy in the Shade

showed up with guns. Mom called it a faith-based initiative. Anyway, it'll be on TV tonight! I bet we get to see Uncle Mike on TV slapping the cuffs on someone! Mike will step on their Twinkies! Those Sowers will be toadmeat on a stick!"

"How do Sower kids get along in school?"

"Heck, the old guys don't allow kids to come to school. That's how they stay brainwashed. It's like a prison out there. Byron that you work for at the gas station, he was a Sower but he started to have his own ideas. They kicked him out, shunned him is what they call it, because he wanted to let the kids go to school. He's been out a long time."

Sandy paused to fiddle with the handcuffs below the desktop.

"The bosses make up reasons to kick younger men out," he continued. "It's so they can have the women for themselves. Mom says most religions don't let you think for yourself, but the Sowers are the worst. The kids can't watch TV, can't play video games—nothin'."

"Doesn't sound like there are a lot of laughs in Sowerland."

"They probably think laughing's a sin," Sandy replied. "The only church I'd ever join is The Church of the Flying Spaghetti Monster. Have you heard of it?"

"No," I confessed.

"There's a whole book about how the universe was designed by the Flying Spaghetti Monster. The book is a joke about Intelligent Design, and Mom says they should teach it in schools."

Then he interrupted the discussion to tug at something behind the desk.

"Boogers!" he exclaimed before slipping into a protracted growl.

"What's the matter?"

"Nothing," he said, his face catching fire like a sunset.

After the Floods

"Boogers!" he muttered, along with that odd phrase about loud crines. He continued the secret tug-of-war.

I stepped behind the desk. "Got yourself handcuffed to the desk?"

"I guess so."

"Well, where's the key?"

"It was on the desk," he said uncertainly.

"When."

"Before."

"Before what?"

"If I knew before what, I'd probably know where I put it. Duh!"

I found the key on the floor and knelt down to unlock the cuffs.

"No," he protested. "Lemme do it. I need to learn how to get out of cuffs fast! You never know."

As he tried the key, cranking his head this way and that, he asked if I knew what happens to babies that come when dads marry their own daughters. I said that he'd better tell me his version.

"Sometimes the babies come out with parts all stuck together," he explained enthusiastically. "Mom saw one where the legs were stuck together so it was really like just one big leg with two little feet on the bottom. Sometimes it's not even a human that comes out! It's just a bunch of goo with an eyeball floating in it, or half a brain!"

I was silent as he looked at me expectantly.

"So when someone talks about Intelligent Design," he went on, "Mom gets mega-mad. Mom says they've had things at the hospital that even the oldest doctor never saw before! Things that weren't designed right, if you see what I mean."

Billy in the Shade

"Your mom told you that?"

"When I ask, she says never mind. But I hear her talking on the phone to her girlfriends. That's what she calls them even though they're all nearly thirty. Mom says the Sowers are all confuzzled from nutty beliefs."

"They don't understand why the babies are messed up?" I asked, stretching my neck to get a look at the handcuff situation.

"The older men say it's because the woman sinned. Those guys never took Biology, and they're all lagged up. All the older kids say lagged up now, which means dumb in spades. Uncle Mike says the Sowers can't even find their butts with a searchlight."

Sandy paused to giggle at the image.

"The ones I saw had the cell-phone technology down," I said, remembering the spooky encounter with the gravediggers.

"Mom says the Sowers show how dangerous belief is," he continued. "She says we should try not to have beliefs, and if we do we should keep quiet about them. She gets really mad when people start talking about their beliefs like it's something to be proud of."

Sandy paused as the key clicked and the cuffs sprung open. "You don't have beliefs, do you?" he asked.

"I believe you just got yourself out of those cuffs," I said.

"That ain't a belief. That's a fact." He displayed the open cuffs and smiled. "Mom says we ought to stick with the facts, and when there's stuff we don't know we should just be okay with not knowing. Don't go inventing myths and beliefs."

I wasn't comfortable with the topic of goofy beliefs, given my Curly-Larry-and-Moe days in New Orleans, so I improvised with, "Looks like the Sowers' family tree hasn't got branches."

Sandy giggled and said, "Yeah, it's like, *hey sis, how's our baby doing?* That's Uncle Mike's joke."

After the Floods

"Anyone give you permission to grow up so fast?" I asked. "You've had a mega-rad education for a ten-year-old."

"Eleven. That's what Mom says, only she says warp-rad. Mom says I'll either be a genius or a lunatic when I grow up. I think I'll be a genius on the cover of *TV Guide.* Do you like dogs?"

"I guess so."

"Mudface is knocked up. That's what Uncle Mike calls it. It means she's gonna have pups. Want a pup?"

"I love puppies," I said. "I could just eat them."

A tune came from somewhere in his clothing. His hand went in after the merry melody and emerged with a cell phone, which he poked with a thumb and then pressed to his ear.

"Sandman here . . . Mom! Guess what! I locked myself in handcuffs and lost the key . . . Bill found it. Mom! What comes after ten? Onety-one, get it? It should be onety-one to fit with the rest of the numbers . . . Yeah, Bill's here and I told him he's too young, but he loves you anyway . . . Sure, just a minute." He lowered the cell and asked me if I could drive him home. "Yeah, he says he can. He says he even learned to drive on real streets in Nawlins. That's how they say New Orleans . . . Okay. And I'll tell him to buy cookies at Birdie's Bakery. Let's have lemonade."

Sandy couldn't find his Twins cap, and I heard more about boogers. I spotted the cap under the desk and we headed out, telling the sentry at the door that we were going home. Sandy stooped to pick up a black feather before tumbling into the Civic.

In the car Sandy said, "Be sure and tell Mom I had my nap today. I was taking it just before you came. I'm always supposed to take a nap after I'm up late with Uncle Mike. Mom has a bubble-gum addiction, so we gotta stop at Moody's for her fix."

Billy in the Shade

Sandy explained that Birdie herself isn't working in the bakery this summer—something about becoming a dancer. But a pleasant woman served us from behind a counter lavishly stacked with oozing cream puffs, corpulent long johns, glazed donuts, and a dozen other delights that sent The Sandman into serious indecision. She smiled as she inserted two of this and two of that into a paper bag, her eyes twinkling from a face that was a batter of powder and lotion.

"What lags me up," I said after the gum stop at Moody's, "is, are you asking me to tell your mom a belief about that nap or are we sticking with the facts? And how can the nap be a fact to me if I wasn't there to hear you snore? Maybe what's a fact to you can only be a belief to me."

"I'll tell her about the nap myself," Sandy replied after a troubled pause.

"Does this have anything to do with that car accident?"

"What car accident?"

"The one that knocked the truth out of you."

"That was a lie," Sandy said. "I lost the truth after the spacemen kidnapped me for experiments. As far as the nap goes, just be okay with what you don't know."

"Gotchya," I said, hooking a Lewis onto the county road. The helicopters had disappeared, and the summer sky was clear and blue. Sandy punched on the radio and began searching for an acceptable station.

"Every other station is religion," he said. "They're taking over, like in The Body Snatchers, only it's brain snatchers now.

• • •

After the Floods

Clear and blue skies are good, God, except I was still doofus enough to think You might jot a few ideas for me in the clouds. Maybe it's that Your ideas are, like, too huge and rad and all to fit into Earth words. Maybe it's like trying to text-message *War and Peace*, or to catch the smell of a rose in a butterfly net. I'm trying to give You the benefit of the doubt, but I'm starting to think I'm on my own down here, or that it's just me and Sister Ann, know what I mean? I'm roaming, Man, and the connection's bad. I've gotten further chatting with cats.

Passing thought: Try the Miracle Ear. It worked for my granddad.

P.S. What's with the mockingbirds in Minnesota? You moving the furniture around? Redecorating?

The Night of the Sowers

To: God
From: Billy B.
CC: Sister Ann
Re: Your followers, my friends

As we rode along, Sandy occupied himself with working the feather into his cap. With our pastries from Birdie's and Siiri's bubble-gum fix from Moody's, we pulled into Siiri's driveway and parked behind Macro's copmobile. The two of them sat on lawn chairs in the yard near the promiscuous Mudface, who dozed in a splash of shade by the well. You wouldn't have thought that Saint Bob and his deranged zealots were prowling in nearby trees with guns propped in deformed arms. Sandy

Billy in the Shade

flung himself from my Civic and raced to Siiri, who stood and then knelt for one of those hugs people do as worry leaks away.

"Did you guys get shot at?" Sandy asked, breaking free of his mother to roust Mudface with some vigorous petting. "Did you kick their butts, Uncle Mike?"

"One nurse got shot," Mike said, "but she'll be okay. Two of the Sower Storm Troopers won't be okay."

Siiri's face glistened with tears as she walked over to hug Sandy again.

"It's so awful," she said, "so goddamned crazy. How do life's rocks and rapids produce people like that?"

"Well," Mike sighed, "when you don't have TV you have to make your own fun."

No one laughed.

We went inside, where Siiri had arranged a platter of sandwiches, glasses, and a pitcher of lemonade on a coffee table in front of the sofa. Sandy proudly set our bag of pastries and cookies (the brown stains indicating freshness, as that radio guy says) on a book next to the pitcher and handed his mom her bubble gum from Moody's. The book, with its image of a dark flag on the cover, looked suspiciously familiar.

"We've been making groceries," Sandy announced. "That's what they say down in Nawlins. They don't say shopping for groceries. I think some of the cookies broke when Mom and me were hugging. They'll taste better that way, with all the love crunched in."

Siiri made a move to hug him again, but he ducked behind the sofa.

"Plenty of time for that later," Sandy said. "I don't want gum all over my feather. But don't forget to save the baseball cards! If you'd been doing it all along, we'd be rich. I keep telling you."

After the Floods

"You certainly do," Siiri affirmed. "Now go wash up. Those hands are scary."

"I'll make groceries disappear fast," Mike said, settling deep into the sofa and reaching for a sandwich. "I gotta head back to the office in half an hour. I want you to stay here tonight," he added, eying me over a bun stuffed with tuna salad. "Things might not be quiet for a while. State Troopers, along with a few National Guard backups, are starting to surround the Sowers about now, blocking roads and so on."

"The Sowers will try to ram right through the roadblocks in their pickups!" Sandy exclaimed, returning from the kitchen and plopping down by Mike. "They've got pickups filled with explosives, just like in Iraq! It'll be a huge catastrophuck!"

"Don't say phuck, Sandy," his mother said.

"I can't say anything."

"Who told you that?" Mike asked. He was on edge.

"A little bird," Sandy replied. "A crow," he added, glancing at me.

"Well," Mike said, relaxing a bit, "we don't know what to expect, so we just gotta be careful. They've got eighty acres or more, and some of them could seep away into the woods or neighboring property tonight."

He paused to make a good bit of the sandwich disappear.

"The men will be arrested and sorted out, but trouble could run through the night. Tomorrow the women and children get taken to temporary housing facilities. Tonight, we'll have patrol cars out on the streets in town and on the county road, so things should be safe here."

"Mudface will chew butt if they come here. They'll be toast."

Sandy's words came from a mouth overflowing with chips like spelunkers emerging from a muddy cave. Then he picked up

150

Billy in the Shade

the bag from the bakery, leaving the glossy cover of the familiar book shining up at me. He plunged a hand into the bag.

"What you digging for in there?" Mike asked.

"A whole one. *Duh*!"

"*Duh* isn't always cool," Mike pointed out, working his shoulders for kinks.

"I can't say anything."

"And what's the long-range plan?" Siiri asked, pressing her load of bubble gum to the side of her plate and reaching for a sandwich.

"The county prosecutor tells me that enough women, and some of the guys who were booted out over the years, will testify. So the plan is the leaders do major jail time. I figure we got a 60% chance. Of course there'll be religious freedom issues and the bullshit will fly, by which I mean bull doodies, Sandy."

"The bull doodies," Siiri mused. "They don't just drop, do they?"

"You could make a cartoon about what everyone says at the trial," Sandy offered. "The cartoon would be a room full of doodies with wings on them flying around like hummingbirds. If I draw it, do ya think it could get in *The Weekly Peep?*"

We all looked at our young genius for a moment.

"Yes, I do," Mike said. "It'd be the most sensible thing Ferguson has printed in a while."

"What ever happened to religion being about kindness and love, about social justice and peace?" Siiri wondered. "Anyone who's bragging about his religion these days is just out to silence this group or control that group. It's shameful. I could scream."

"Yeah, it's a mess," Macro said, "always has been. I wasn't much of a student, as Dad liked to point out at the supper table, but weren't people killing each other over religion right from the get-go?"

151

After the Floods

"Don't forget spousal abuse, sexism, and racism," Siiri added. "Those are things Guidry exposes in his book." She nodded toward the glistening book on the table as she pried the wad of gum from her plate.

"I'll never have a religion," Sandy said proudly, reaching for the cookie bag again. "I'm gonna tell everyone that if you don't know how the world got here, then you don't know. You shouldn't go making up stories and then getting in big fights about it."

He lifted a peanut butter cookie and dunked it dramatically into his lemonade, a theatrical finale to his speech. The cookie crumbled. "Boogers!" he complained.

"You say boogers a lot," I observed.

"I like boogers," he replied, adjusting his baseball cap and eying me slyly. "I could just eat them."

I stayed quiet though the exchange about religion gone astray, not mentioning my experiences with scientific faith implantation in New Orleans, and I felt ashamed of my silence. Siiri, Sandy, and Macro Mike were morphing into a warm, new family for me. I didn't want to have secrets from them, but I didn't want to appear foolish, either. And foolish is how that whole thing about medically induced religion was starting to seem.

"Gotta run," Mike said, standing slowly and working his neck and shoulders about. Dark pouches had formed around his eyes, and he hadn't shaved in a day and a half.

"You need sleep," Siiri said.

"We got a cot I can stretch out on. I'll be fine. If I don't see you again today, be sure to keep the doors locked and the yard light on tonight. We got guys patrolling the county road, and if you think you see or hear anything, and I'm talking *anything* Siiri, just call and I'll have someone there in a minute."

The three of us cleaned up, Siiri popping bubbles and trying to

152

Billy in the Shade

be cheerful. Back in the family room, Siiri picked up the glistening book, called *Religion's Dark Shadow,* which had been written by my old college roommate, John Guidry.

"Ever read this?" she asked, waving it in the air. "It mentions some nutjobs down in New Orleans, and it debunks idiots like the Sowers. He points out that everyone's going all public and pushy about their religion, but it's considered rude for the rest of us to respond. He says we need to speak up, to say that belief is not knowledge and that 'faith is a form that fantasy takes.' A great phrase, no?"

She paused to gaze at the book like it was *The Holy Bible,* and then she continued to chant the praises of the great author whose Jockeys and smelly socks had decorated my life for over a year before our views hit a fork in the road. Eventually, she slipped the book into an empty space in the bookcase to doze with the likes of Gary Snyder, Bertrand Russell, and *The Church of the Flying Spaghetti Monster.*

"I read part of it in the New Orleans paper," I managed to say, wondering if I should go home and bury myself in the Sower cemetery. At least I hadn't been mentioned by name in the *Times-Picayune.*

That afternoon, under a bright sun, we put a new bolt in the pump handle, cut the grass with an ancient, human-powered mower, and slapped white paint on a few yards of the fence. Bird's circled above us. Then Sandy and I got in a water fight. He wielded the hose that stretched from the house, and I dodged and zigged with a bucket from the well.

Siiri removed a blade of grass from her mouth and waded in shouting, "Order in the court!"

"This ain't no court!" Sandy retorted. "This is a battlefield!"

Squirrels scampered, Mudface barked, a bald eagle looked

After the Floods

down as he floated beneath a cloud, and leaves whispered in the trees. Later, curled on the sofa as the air outside darkened and the windows turned to mirrors, we watched a *Seinfeld* re-run over burgers, chips and Cokes.

"Wanna watch a *Buffy* before we go to bed?" Siiri asked.

"I could hump that!" Sandy responded.

"That's not a good expression for a dude of your years," his mom advised, a little tiredness creeping into her voice.

"Why?"

"Take it on faith," she said.

"Faith?"

"Well, take it from your mom."

"Okay."

They had the entire *Buffy, the Vampire Slayer* collection on DVD, and an episode was picked at random.

"Did you see the one where they all have to sing their lines?" Sandy asked as the screen warned us about the various ways we could be jailed for using the DVD. "It's awesome, except Willow can't sing."

"I like the one where no one can talk at all," Siiri said. "Those gliding ghouls are *so* creepy!"

"I got some catching up to do," I said, referring to something that had just occurred in the opening scene, "but it's neat how the vampires turn into dust when they're stabbed. No one has to call Waste Management. They don't even have to sweep the floor."

Sandy snickered, and then he said, "My favorite character is Willow. She's so funny. I liked it when she was with Oz. It's sad, though, when she turns into an evil witch. But that's not until season six. Before that she was a cute witch just messing around. And Oz was so good when he found out he was a werewolf. He woke up naked in the park and just said *hmmm*."

Billy in the Shade

"I like Spike," Siiri offered, as the blond and very drunk vampire tumbled out of a car and into the lives of the young Sunnydale team. "He's a yummy bad boy!"

"Maybe you should be bad like Spike," Sandy suggested, eying me up and down. "Get a long, black leather coat, bleach your hair, and lose your soul. Then Mom will forget you're too young."

"Why didn't I think of that?" I asked.

"You're lagged up about women?" Sandy suggested as he began to pull off his shoes and socks.

"Shut up, please." That was Siiri snipping the thread.

Then it was bedtime. I'd sleep on the couch downstairs, and Siiri and Sandy had bedrooms above.

"Don't get the googley-moogleys in your eyes," Sandy warned has he climbed the stairs. I assume he was talking about sleep-chunks.

"Don't let the Sowers bite," I replied.

"Before you hop in bed, mister, I want you to floss between those toes," Siiri said, starting up the stairs behind him. Then she paused and glanced back at me.

"Do they really say *make groceries* in Louisiana? It seems so odd."

"They sure do, sha," I answered.

"Sha?"

"It's Cajun—a good word, I promise. You hear it under moonlight on the bayou."

"I'll trust you on that. Goodnight, Boichild."

"Tootles, sha."

When Sandy came out of the bathroom, I heard him ask his mother if he could sleep with her.

"I'm so glad you offered," Siiri replied. "I'll feel a lot safer being with you, and I'll get to see if you actually sleep all night in that Twins cap."

155

After the Floods

"Nah, it comes off when I roll around," Sandy replied. "Plus I don't want to wreck the feather. Mudface, come. We're gonna protect Mom tonight."

Claws scampered on the floor, leaving, I imagined, a regiment of toy Spidermen, Tomb Raiders, and Hobbits to negotiate the night for themselves in Sandy's room. Then Siiri's door clicked shut.

• • •

I lay awake on the couch for a long time as the wind made worried sighs in the trees, not worried about flooding or global warming, but about what a sad old place the world is thanks to butt-ugly nastiness and arrogance. I knew Siiri was right to say that religion has become a tool of the vicious, that the message of love isn't what we hear anymore when fundamentalists obscure the sun. Hatred is setting up shop in downtown Christianity, just like it did in Islam. It's the fractal thing. Sometimes it's beautiful how everything is like everything else, but at other times it feels like craziness.

Memory and forgetting are a single, breathing organ, like the sea folding things under and flinging things up. That night I remembered Kyle, my friend who went insane in New Orleans. Perhaps a drizzle off of Lake Pontchartrain, turning the evening to damp ashes, would sadden him. He slept on my couch once, and I heard him cry long into the night, his sobs slowing from time to time like rain ending. Another time he tried to cut himself with a knife from my kitchen.

His parents had been meth-heads and tossed him out when he was ten, his dad tucking a few dollars in his shirt pocket and saying *start walking*. I wondered where Kyle had gotten to now in the general dream of things, and I worried that the past was

Billy in the Shade

slipping away and that the real places and people I'd known were now just shadows behind me.

Later I remembered old Ralph Leavitt, a guy about eighty who'd died in New Orleans. He'd been part of the little silly religion that I'd joined. I thought about him and about how easily life wanders away. I think that when someone dies, a bit of meaning leaves the world with him.

Every person gives meaning to special things in his life, like the meaning of the little objects that Ralph kept in his cabinet or the meaning of his favorite tunes. And all of the other things with private associations, rain tapping on a roof or the scent of a favorite flower in a garden, can never be exactly the same for anyone else. So when a person dies, the meaning he's given to things dies too.

A voice told me that truth and meaning are wanderers, living here and there, sometimes in a church, sometimes in a book, a river, or a person. And as soon as you're sure you know where they are, they're gone and you have to become a wanderer too.

I thought that I heard tapping sounds outside, and then I caught a fast pitch from Sandy, but the next pitch was wide and I fell because Kyle and Ralph had tied my shoelaces together. Sandy moonwalked away on a single leg with ten toes. Recess was over and the other kids went inside, but my legs were stuck together and I was paralyzed. I had lost my cap. Cop cars circled the cemetery as dead people clawed up from graves, pawed mud from their rotting faces, and turned toward me, their ponytails hanging to the ground.

Siiri made a distant clatter, and the dead guys faded. Then she was beside me offering a mug of coffee and lefsa with brown sugar rolled inside. A slice of morning sun slid under the window shade, and upstairs Sandy discussed puppy names with Mudface.

157

After the Floods

The morning tried to be cheerful, but my dream had made me feel like a deserter, what with Dad being sick and all.

The Haircut of the Future

To: Sister Ann
From: Billy B.
CC:
Re: Grooming today

The Sowers' ship of fate still plunges through the rough waters of the daily news. *The Weekly Peep* generates tides of indignation, and Cold Beak even made the national news. I suppose the story will soon be lost in history. Last week, as the excitement cooled, Siiri grabbed a couple of days off from the hospital to drive to Minneapolis with Sandy for an urban holiday.

He'd romp through Valley Fair, an amusement park outside of the city near the Minnesota River, and then spend two hundred dollars at Mall of America. I was invited to tag along, and during some down time on Saturday, as the two of them cruised the Mall, I slipped out of my room at HoJo's for a haircut. Great Snips beckoned from down a sunny strip mall next to the motel.

A thirty-something mimbo with boo-coo tattoos and metal pellets in his eyebrows smiled from behind a computer at the front counter.

"Hi there," he said. "I'm Renaldo. May I have your phone and social security numbers?"

"Actually, that's private information," I replied.

"Technically, but hel-*lo*! We want to pull up your file each

Billy in the Shade

time you sashay in. It helps us know you so that we can meet your every social and grooming need as well and fully as possible. We want to serve you in each and every way we can. It's like, Great Snips isn't just about cutting hair. That's so totally last week. We offer complete and detailed lifestyle guidance. Your appearance is our passion and profession."

He may have delivered "passion" with a slight leer, but I wasn't sure.

"Okay," I said, "but I don't want a lot of guidance and advice, and I can just tell the man or woman behind the counter or desk how I want it cut and trimmed when I come in. It's no big and expanding deal."

Renaldo of the Jeweled Brows had a ponytail that reminded me of Kyle. He smiled patiently, also a bit like Kyle, and I really hoped and wished that he'd stop reminding me of friends and acquaintances.

Instead he replied, "I speak in pairs for emphasis. But you see, if we know about you we can recommend things that you might not have thought of—skin products, conditioners, styling alternatives. If you're gay, for instance, Great Snips knows what the latest styles are for the fashionable queer in the urban scene. Are you gay?"

His ringed fingers hovered above the keyboard.

"No."

"May I just enter straight then? Or would you prefer our neutral category? We have excellent suggestions for young men who find themselves betwixt and between. There's a new scent, for example, that arouses sexual interest in either gender. Most scents are gender specific. Did you know that? This is the sort of information we have. We serve our customers one person at a time."

After the Floods

"I really don't . . ."

"Do you often masturbate in public places? Our cameras in Men's down the hall caught you in a stall a few minutes ago. Wank, wank, wank!" His ponytail bobbed with each wank.

(I was only scratching, Sister. Honest!)

"We have some excellent hair styles and skin products designed especially for people who like *it* in the tea room," he continued. "The air quality in most tea rooms presents particular grooming issues. You probably wouldn't have known that if I hadn't raised the topic. See how it works? Are you familiar with the term *tea room*?"

"Yeah, but . . ."

"With my help, you'll have it made in the shade, socially speaking. *Made in the shade* is something my father used to say. Have you heard it before?"

It was weird to hear that one of my own father's expressions had also been used by Renaldo's dad. It seemed like a violation of my past and an affront to privacy, as though my very special life had been shown to be generic.

"Yeah," I said. "I also remember *in like Flynn*."

"You're not from around here, are you? May I type in Southerner?"

"Why not? Will it help me get a haircut before midnight?"

"Patience is a virtue. Are you religious? Southern Baptist? Do you handle snakes?"

"Never touched one."

"Ever dream about snakes? Dreams are important indicators of unconscious grooming preferences."

"My hair is growing as we talk. Styles are changing."

"Where in the South are you from?"

"New Orleans."

160

Billy in the Shade

"Louisiana!" he cooed, sliding up the scale on the second syllable like a mourning dove.

"Yeah, that's where they keep New Orleans."

"Ah yes, Sin City." A faraway look clung to Renaldo's face like shrink wrap. "I remember the time Danny and I . . . But I digress."

"I'm a digresser, too. We have one thing in common."

"Hmm," he mused, perhaps intending to look for other points of contact. Instead, he went back to his first love. "Great Snips hasn't expanded into the South yet. We only operate in the more progressive Northern cities. As far as New Orleans is concerned, we are still the glistening future." He paused for my reply, but I left him hanging.

"Our customer profiles," he eventually continued, "allow our computers to generate the perfect modes of grooming and accessories for your lifestyle. We only share the information with businesses that support our goals of serving your personal image in the most helpful and efficient ways possible. That's why we get IT done before each stylistic procedure."

"No thanks. I'm avoiding Tomorrow Land."

"You'll be much happier when you stop fighting it, the future I mean." Renaldo leaned across the counter confidentially. "Go with the flow, you bad boy! You're in good hands with Great Snips. Now then," he said, going back to his computer, "I need to know your monthly income, your local bank, and your mother's maiden name."

I made up some lies, and by sunset I was seated before a mirror that reflected Renaldo flourishing the inevitable cape like a bullfighter and slinging it around my neck. For the next fifteen minutes, as the scissors flew about my head and Renaldo bent this way and that, I learned much more than I wanted to know about his and Danny's sexual romp through my home city. He

161

After the Floods

even recounted, replete with snickers and sighs, a sordid scene of fumbling pleasure in the dim light of the 'tea room' at The Seven Seas, a French Quarter bar where Kyle and I had often gone to play chess during the year before Katrina.

Renaldo finished our little session with a lingering shoulder rub as he smiled at me affectionately in the mirror, the metal in his eyebrows seeming to wink like a Christmas light. Then, as his brush flicked the final fallen hairs from my neck and shirt, I remarked that there was clearly no privacy left in his colorful world.

"Sweetheart," he said, somehow I had made the leap to sweetheart, "there's no privacy in your world either. You just don't know it yet."

Then, as I paid him at the computer, I tried to imagine Carlson slapping a walleye down on Renaldo's counter as he had on Gopher's.

As a parting gift, Renaldo added, "I know that you lied to me about your mom's maiden name. Tootles, you naughty puppy."

Tootles! Kyle is the only other human who has ever said "tootles" to me. It was a deeply disturbing deja thing. He was stealing words and phrases right out of my own life! Then Renaldo was a Key West cruiser waving goodbye to me, his latest lost sailor. I got back to HoJo's just in time to see Siiri and Sandy unloading armfuls of packages from the car.

"What goodies has Mall of America yielded?" I asked as they dumped their purchases on their bed.

"That's private information, Buster," Siiri said.

"Yeah, none of your business, Gumbo Man, except for this one," Sandy said, digging into a large bag. "It's a jacket for the fall. Mom bought it for me at The Gap!"

"It's banging gear! You'll knock them dead, Sandman. The ladies will handle you with their eyes."

Billy in the Shade

"If I ever open a store for puppy clothes," he said proudly, "I'll call it The Yap."

"Yeah?" Siiri retorted. "Well, if I open a singing school for puppies, I'll call it Great Yips!"

Sandy's hair received a quick, motherly brush as he gave me the "glance expectant," as I imagine my seventeenth-century ancestors called it.

"You drawing a blank, cowboy?" Siiri asked.

My "yup," forming a brilliant declension from their "yap" and "yip," passed unappreciated. People miss so much.

"Yesss!" Sandy shouted, pumping his fist like Tiger Woods.

I tossed an optimistic eye at the other secrets sprawled about on the bed's acreage. My birthday was coming up, so it had to be booty for me. I smiled and offered to buy dinner.

"Sure," Siiri said. "Sandy, help me move the presents for Uncle Mike out of the way."

"Can you get that haircut fixed before we go?" Sandy asked, turning to grin at me.

"You're pushing it, Sandman," I replied, going after him with monster claws raised.

"Boys! Order in the court!" Siiri shouted.

Sandy dodged around the bed and then cried uncle, and I headed back to my room, squeezing by the inevitable housekeeping cart piled with sheets and towels.

The Mirror Phase that led me, back in May, to my first Minnesota haircut amid the splendor of Gopher's hunting magazines and spittoons, had passed. Nonetheless, as I dressed for our trek to Ruby Tuesday, I checked out my new do. The famous Boichild sideburns, as described in Grandpa's *Chronicles*, had been pruned beyond recognition, and clearly I should have kept Renaldo's assortment of tools away from my eyebrows. Either

After the Floods

Renaldo was just a Gopher with internet access, or he'd dorked me on purpose, unless of course his reverie of the tea room had swamped his concentration.

Maybe I shouldn't have lied about my favorite show tune. Honestly, Sis, I don't even like *Peter Pan*. Oh well.

· · ·

Hey Sis, I know you don't want to get too personal, but what color is your hair? I'd like to have a mental picture. It's why the old painters did so many angels, to have a picture to go with their beliefs. Only I want a picture to go with the facts. You wouldn't need to be real specific. You could just say light or dark, if it's a privacy issue.

Billy Gives God an Earful

To: God
From: Billy B.
CC: Sister Ann
Re: Why I'm pissed

I'm tired of waiting to hear from You. Who do You think You are? In a day or two You'll be off the team. It'll be all Sister Ann. If You do decide to email me, be sure to write *From God* on the subject line. You'd be surprised how much SPAM we get from idiots.

By the way, I read that there are little parasites in African rivers that crawl into children's urethras when they pee in the rivers. Very painful results. What were You thinking when You planned that? And there's a worm that only mates in a hippopotamus's

Billy in the Shade

asshole. Is this, like, Intelligent Design? Were You and the angels smoking something? And then there's Iraq. Terrorism. Birth defects. The electoral college.

You got some explaining to do, Mister.

Dusty

To: Sister Ann
From: Billy Boy
CC: Dad, Wherever You Are
Re: Time

Sister Ann, sometimes, as I lie in bed at night in the woods, the wind in the trees makes the sound of pages turning, and then, just before sleep, the book opens to a page of my life. Last night I remembered Dusty.

• • •

When I was a kid we had a Shih Tzu named Dusty. He looked like Oscar the Grouch, but he was really sweet. I'd walk him on Chestnut Street, sometimes with Dad and Mom, other times just me and Dusty. We trudged for many blocks through summer afternoons when the New Orleans air was like warm Jello. He had trouble focusing on business, poop and pee business. He'd roll on dead squirrels, or he'd carry a dead crow from under our porch to the foot of Mrs. Ferre's crepe myrtle.

Often after a walk, we'd find Dusty on the sofa with a spider dangling from his lips. Dad said that Dusty's job had to do with dead things, rubbing them, sniffing them, moving them about, and generally imposing his own personality on the leavings of

After the Floods

"time's crescent blade." That was Dad's phrase. Dad had a few poems he had written tucked away in a drawer.

Then one morning toward the end of September—school was a couple of weeks old and the air was turning cooler—I padded to the front of our shotgun house in my pajamas like it was just another day. In life, Dusty had paws as soft as pussy willows, but that morning Dusty was on the sofa stiff as fuzzy steel. You could have pounded nails with Dusty.

My powers in the art of lachrymation were well established. There wasn't a kid at Country Day who dared compete with me. But that morning I entered new territory. The house became a disaster zone under a missile barrage of soggy handkerchiefs. One landed on the ceiling fan. Mom flipped the switch, and we watched it fly off into a potted plant, balled up like a grenade. My tanks had burst, and my parents marveled at my endless supply of drizzle.

The weird part was that my awareness of my crying power irritated me. I knew that I had a world record in sight, and I began to pace myself, slowing my sniffles to a jog and then accelerating with blinding speed. I was more focused on the record than on poor Dusty's decision to join the dead things he'd been so managerial about. My crying became insincere, but my anger at my insincerity only served to initiate a new round of high-decibel wailing and spraying. Now I was crying because I was an insincere crier. I was an actor finding a way to *make* myself cry. It was like I was cheating, and even my anger about being a cheater helped me to cheat all the more.

Many years later, I realized that I had simply exhibited a familiar design flaw in the species, the way two levels of awareness or focus interfere. It's like when, before cable TV, there'd sometimes be two different stations showing on the screen at the same time.

Billy in the Shade

Anyhow, eventually Dad flapped into the room in swim fins and a snorkel mask. He pulled up the mask and said, "Good job, Sport. The house is submerged." I smiled, and two months later we got a golden retriever.

Dad was a good friend. I'm worried about his heart, and the last time we talked on the phone he sounded confused.

• • •

Maybe it happened that way, but memories are pretty unreliable. They are like those images of the world as they wobble away in your head just after your eyelids close. I think that I'm afraid to grow old, and sometimes I wish that I were back in my past. It's as though road signs leading home have been washed away in the drifting of things. Or maybe the signs are still there, but home itself has floated away, like truth. Sister, can you tell me why I'm sad now, when things are going so well with Siiri and Sandy? Why does happiness always have a shadow? Is there something wrong with me, or did God make us on purpose to be lost?

Loaves and Walleyes

To: Sister Ann
From: Billy B.
CC:
Re: Carlson's fat ass

On the drive back to Cold Beak from my encounter with the stylin' Renaldo, I made a date with Siiri and Sandy for the Friday Night Fish Fry at Loaves and Fishes, a brass-and-rope place out by Lake Dakota, a few miles north of town. Cold Beak's restau-

167

After the Floods

rants are united in the cause of eliminating all but the most cautious rumor of flavor from the omelets, the soups, the meatballs and spaghetti, and whatever else they get their hands on. There's a new restaurant called The Phoenix that is supposed to be better, but I haven't tried it.

Not wanting to become lost on our first official date, I drove out to the lake for lunch on Wednesday to check out Loaves and Fishes.

You park in a gravel lot, enter the front door, and turn either right or left, unless you prefer to blunder ahead into the kiosks selling the *Weekly Peep* (which I hear is going to change its name to something less silly) and the *Minneapolis Star Tribune*. A right turn means that you intend to knock a few back, maybe watch a Twins or Vikings game on the TV mounted high at the end of the bar, and perhaps fill an ash tray or two. A left turn means food served on tables made from logs split in two and shellacked.

I took a table looking out on the lake. The restaurant was about twenty feet above water level, and the view out to an island, with a few boats here and there on sun-dashed water, was what they want you to think northern Minnesota is all about— all spruce, cedar, and pine, all rippling blue water, all cabins, boats, and canoes.

I sat for a long while with my hand on the menu, finally becoming aware of a waitress standing by the table. She had one of those pads with green lines that waitresses have clutched since Noah docked on a hill. Her name tag said Sheri, and she resembled Siiri.

"Oops," I said. "I got stoned on the view. What's good for lunch?"

"Well," she smiled, twirling her pencil absently, "I like the walleye sandwich. We make the bread fresh. Or you can get the

Billy in the Shade

whole walleye dinner with a salad, baked potato, and a vegetable. We've also got hamburgers, brats, and pork chops. And there's soup. If it were Monday, you could order the walleye hot dish."

"Alas."

"Yes, alas it's Wednesday. But there might be some lutefisk left from the party last night. I could check." Something in Sheri's expression said the lutefisk sucked.

"Isn't that the stuff you put under the porch to keep the skunks away?" I asked.

"It's been tried," she said, her eyes twinkling, "but then you have the problem of keeping the Norwegians away."

I smiled appreciatively and ordered the sandwich and soup.

"What kind of soup? We have . . ."

"Surprise me."

"Lunch on the edge, is it?"

"Oh yeah, I was born in Edge City. Is the walleye out of this lake?"

"Commercial fishing isn't allowed on these lakes. We get it fresh form Canada. There's a local guy named Bob Carlson who keeps trying to sell to us. Can't get it through his head that he's illegal. Want something to drink?"

"Coke's good. You're not Siiri Elden's sister, are you?"

"Nope, sorry."

"No problem. It's that fractal thing."

"Sorry about that. My dad had laser surgery last year. Sees like a hawk now."

"Maybe I'll look into it."

"I forgot. For that sandwich, we have French bread, Italian, sour dough, or plain old white. In my opinion, sour dough doesn't swim with walleye very well."

After the Floods

"How about French?"

"Excellent choice, Monsieur," she said through lovely lips. "Bowl or cup?"

"Huh?"

"On the soup."

"Oh, cup. Would you *like* to be Siiri Elden's sister?" I asked, thinking, *be still my shorts.* "We're looking to start a family."

"You a leftover Sower been hiding in a ditch?"

"Just a perfectionist."

"It's gonna be a conventional family for me," she said, displaying her engagement ring. "My guy even likes my freckles, so it's a done deal."

"A girl without freckles is like a night without stars."

"Well, you do have potential, especially with that accent. I better get your order."

When Sheri returned with a cup of onion soup and what we would call a walleye po-boy in New Orleans, I mentioned that I'd be in on Friday with Siiri and her son.

"Okay, I'll check them out and tug my ear twice if I decide to join your new family."

"Actually, I was going to ask if I could reserve this table."

"Well, see, my dad owns this place, and he doesn't like the whole idea of reservations. Too snooty. He thinks reservations are for Republicans. You're not Republican, are you?"

"Only in my nightmares."

"That's good. If you get here by five, we can usually give you a table with a good view. Get here at six and you wait in the bar with the 4x4 and biker crowd."

"Roger that."

As I ate, I thought about old Ralph Leavitt and the waitress

Billy in the Shade

he flirted with at Deanie's one night in New Orleans when we were late for the Early Bird. Ralph was decomposing in his tee and jeans, but he still had a proposition for every woman caught by his radar. Then I wondered if the waitress was still slinging oysters and charming customers at Deanie's. Why does every male capable of speech flirt with waitresses? More to the point, would *I* ever settle on being just one person? Is this what that writer meant by the lightness of being?

When I left a half hour later, I nearly collided with Bob Carlson in front of the newspaper kiosks. Bob, who was even larger than I'd remembered from that day at Gopher's, had just squeezed himself out from the smoky, 4x4 side, where the TV flickered and the pinball machine beeped. He contemplated his attack on the outer doorway, holding his notebook in one hand. A ballpoint peeked over the top of an ink-stained shirt pocket.

The dentist's art isn't held in unwarranted esteem around Cold Beak, and Bob's smile revealed a stumbling assortment of nuts and raisins. His chubby face was like a bowl of batter. We'd never been introduced, and I was surprised when he spoke to me.

"Gator," he said. "After you. I gotta plan my moves here . . . too much snacking between gorgings."

"Thanks, Walleye. Take care."

"Yeah," he replied. "I earned that nickname with my idea for a fish economy. Let's have a beer at Moose's sometime. I got notes on another idea here." He waived his notebook. "You can give me feedback."

"You're definitely on," I said, doing my up-beat thing and leaving him to crush his bulk through the outer doorway.

During the drive back to Cold Beak, crawling along the shore of Lake Dakota and then picking it up on the straightaway into

After the Floods

town, I assessed my progress in my new, unintended, born-again life. My friendship with Siiri, Sandy, and Mike was central, but things were brightening on the fringes too.

First, I had an animal name now, which Gopher had thoughtfully logged into the network. Second, a pretty but engaged waitress had flirted with me, sort of. And third, I'd received another invitation to Moose's Pit Stop. All I needed was a solid position in Cold Beak's booming economy. Maybe I could walk huge people around the grounds up at the Birdella Borguson Institute for Fatties, charming them with my accent.

I knew that if I dropped in at Moose's and held forth about The Apostolic Network of Families, my group of religious nutjobs in New Orleans, I'd probably make the Fool of the Week Board on my very first visit. It would be something to tell Kyle about if we ever made contact again. Of course there was bound to be competition from the wily Mr. Carlson. Fools don't take back seats gracefully. But I figured Mike would be ready with the cuffs if events turned sucky. Who knows, maybe I'd get to spend a night in the slammer.

All in all, things were *so* looking up.

· · ·

But I did flirt with Sheri. Why, Sis? Why can't I just be one person, and why is life always changing? Sometimes I think that I'm like a river under my skin. The circumstances outside me are the banks and levees of the river, and when they change I change. In New Orleans I was religious, and around Siiri I'm not. The Billy water is always ready to flow in another direction, and there's nothing inside me that makes me be one particular river.

Billy in the Shade

But I want to be a solid person, not just water ready to spill anywhere. Is there a special character solidifier I don't know about? Your answers have all been pretty good, especially that part about Beano, and now isn't a time to hold back the info.

Puppies, Pastries, and Big, Big Bubbles

To: Sister Ann
From: Billy of the North
CC:
Re: Happiness (?)

My dream last night was a jumble of New Orleans and Cold Beak, of Sowers and hurricanes. Vast clouds circled the drain like suds around a black hole. Crows were everywhere, like black shadows talking. Parts of babies bobbed up from graves in the woods, and corpses floated in Siiri's lawn and down long avenues lined with mangled balconies tearing themselves loose from buildings. On the lawn inside of Loyola University's horseshoe parking lane, a marble arm from the Touchdown Jesus statue lay in the grass. Prayers were smoke billowing from dead mouths at Touchdown's feet. The living hid in the broken branches of live oaks as Sowers looted hospitals and homes. The army came and put us in a giant dome that sank slowly into a river.

The wind sifted softly in the trees outside. Sometimes, for a moment after waking, I don't know who I am, and then reality settles into place. Oh yeah, I was Bill Boichild. I could tell from the crack across the ceiling that I was in my trailer in Cold Beak, Minnesota. The Sowers had been rounded up. Women

After the Floods

and children were in safe houses, and the men were being sorted out in regional jails. Saint Bob was busted, and charges would be filed. Religious freedom would not be the freedom to persecute and enslave. At least not here.

I rolled out of bed and poked around for my celly, which was hiding under an aromatic sock on a chair. I called Siiri to invite myself for breakfast, but instead I got "Sandman here," who told me that Siiri was visiting a friend but would be home by noon. Would I like to come over to see the pups that had arrived in the night? If I decided to go in town first, would I make groceries at Birdie's Bakery?

As I drove the county road, I glanced up the driveway with the Carlson sign, still not knowing if it was the Carlson of the fish economy whom I'd met at Loaves and Walleyes. No, Loaves and Fishes. The driveway disappeared in trees and shadows. All along the road's gentle curves, the mountain ash were heavy with berries. Rain had been below average for the summer, and leaves on the hillside were already showing autumn colors. Soon they would be underfoot, sounding like paper.

Sandy sat in the grass by the well leaning over a bicycle pump, its hose attached to a football. Beyond the fence, a peacock carried its many eyes back into the trees. The yellow, red, and green of the maple reminded me of Coach's Mardi Gras tee. As I climbed out of the Civic, I thought I heard boogers being invoked.

"Need any help?" I asked as I arrived at his side. His trusty baseball cap lay in the grass beside him.

"Nah, I got it now," he proclaimed, yanking the needle from the ball. "Run out for one."

"Can't," I said. "I'm lugging a sack full of donuts."

"With the stains that mean freshness?"

Billy in the Shade

"See for yourself, Sandman. Then let's check out those pups."
I put the sack on the table by the well.

"Come on around back. Mom fixed up a bed in the entry
way. There's seven! They've got some white in them, so Uncle
Mike says he knows who to sue for child support."

Mudface was curled in a large basket filled with pillows, blankets, and seven dappled pups in various stages of squirmy sleep.
She raised her head to greet us, poked one of the pups with her
rubbery nose, and then settled back into her doggy doze.

"So," I asked, "who's the proud papa?"

"It's embarrassing," Sandy said.

"I'm gonna find out. I used to be a detective, you know. My
beat was the seedy underbelly of The Big Easy—the bars, the
dope dens, and the smoky backrooms where vast criminal plots
are hatched."

"Shut up!"

"Really, no doodies. It was back when you were all pacifiers
and footy-jams."

"I never wore footy-jams," Sandy replied indignantly.

"Did too. Your mom has a picture."

"I was drugged."

"She says how cute you were snoring in your footies."

"I never snored."

"Grinding away like an engine trying to start."

"You couldn't detect your nose with a flashlight," he said,
switching the focus back to me.

"Tell me about the daddy dog," I replied.

"Well, it was a Sower dog . . . we think. Mom said she saw
Mudface gambling with him in the woods."

"You mean gamboling?" I asked, thinking I'd misheard.

After the Floods

"No," he said, his look telling me that I was an idiot, "they had a weekly poker game out there. Anyway, pretty soon he started leaving pee-mail on the fence."

"They sound like Romeo and Juliet. So what happened to the dog now that the Sowers are toadmeat?"

"Oh, he still hangs around. We put food and water back by the shed every day. He'll probably end up living here. We'll convert him. Promise not to tell he's a Sower? Mom says we can make him into a heathen again. You do it with treats."

"Create heathens?"

"Train dogs!" he replied, laughing. "Ain't you learned nothin'?"

I promised not to tell about the dog's sordid past, and as we went down the back steps Sandy called, "Ding-dong! Here Ding-dong!" No dog appeared. "He doesn't know his new name. We don't know what he was called when he lived on the fanatic farm, but I call him Ding-dong because he was a Sower and they're all ding-dong."

"Maybe we ought to get back to those donuts before the critters find them," I suggested.

"Good call," Sandy said, bursting into a run. "Last one there fetches the lemonade."

I turned and headed back to the kitchen. Mudface had entered her own doggy Singularity, that event after which all is different, and I paused to give her a scratch behind an ear. The trusty pitcher was, as always, half full in the fridge, and I pulled a couple of paper cups from a dispenser. It was Labor Day. The days had turned cool, and during donuts and lemonade in the shade of the maple I asked The Sandman if he was ready for school.

"In Science we're gonna have a unit on bio-chemistry! I think what's wrong with the Sowers is all brain chemistry. When I

176

Billy in the Shade

grow up, I'm gonna invent drugs to help people get rid of stupid beliefs. I'm gonna have my picture on magazines!"

"You could raise money for a hospital to cure stupid beliefs," I said, realizing for the zillionth time how far I was from fessing up to my own life in New Orleans. Looking to change the subject that I'd raised like an idiot, I asked who Siiri was visiting.

"Her girlfriend, Linda, had a baby," Sandy replied. "Mom calls her a girl even though she's thirty-one. The baby just started to say some words, so Mom rushed over."

"The premier performance. Is the baby saying *for crine out loud*?" I gave him my aren't-I-clever look.

"I don't get it."

"Everyone says that up here," I said. I hate explaining a joke. "I figured maybe it was taught in the crib, for crine out loud. What does *crine* mean, anyway?"

"Crine? It's cry-*ing*, for crying out loud. Don't they have any expressions down South?"

"Sorry. But what's the *for* for? Why *for* crying-out loud?

"It's just what we say. Get over it. Crime-in-Italy!"

"Cry . . . ? Never mind."

Siiri's old Ford Escort crunched into the gravel driveway, and as she climbed out Sandy ran for the usual exchange of hugs. We sat in the shade by the well and the maple, and when Sandy wandered off to check on Mudface and family, Siiri asked me what my plans were now that summer was ending and Cold Beak was safe from Sowers.

"Mike says he's going to need a new assistant. He thinks you'd make a good assistant sheriff. It must be your firm but gentle manner. Maybe that authoritative look in your eye. Go figure. Anyway, he's going to retire in two or three years. He wants to get a teaching certificate and coach football. So you could

After the Floods

probably move right up. That is, if you don't get involved in any goofy cults in the meantime."

In a moment of panic, I was sure that she knew all about New Orleans, and I felt my tongue turning to cement. Two squirrels looped down the tree as they had the day we met, and the power line featured birds like bottles on a shelf.

"I'm sorry," she said, slipping a blade of grass between her teeth. "I can't get the Sowers off my mind. We sent Barbara home today. She's the nurse that got shot. She's up and around, but she'll need some counseling. The woman who came in from the Sower commune had a miscarriage and is also in bad shape in the head."

"I'm glad that the authorities are taking steps," I replied, exorcising the spooky thoughts. "There are a lot of people who can't handle freedom except to abuse it."

Sometimes, when those platitudes rise up like water in the brain, I get this weird feeling that I'm not me. I can't explain. But the panic about being busted had disappeared down the county road, and I told Siiri that Katrina had sent Dad to Houston two years ago, where he stayed with his brother for a while. The stress of Katrina had caused a heart attack, but now he was back in NOLA (New Orleans Louisiana), and then I explained that I'd be going back there too for a while. Dad was old, and it was time for me to be useful.

"Dad lives by Audubon Park now, and luckily that area didn't flood much. But the store on Canal Street took some flooding from Katrina, and he hasn't been able to sell it. I need to help him . . . and just to be with him for a while, although in another way going back seems like climbing into my own shadow."

"Are your other friends okay in New Orleans?"

Skipping the embarrassing parts, I said that I'd stayed in touch with my old high school football coach and that his

Billy in the Shade

daughter had taken him to South Carolina, where she and her new husband were settling in a McMansion by a golf course. To the extent that our hospital project had anything like direction, Coach had been its leader.

"Coach was stressed even before Katrina, and now it's worse. His mind is heading North."

"We saying going South," Siiri pointed out.

"Such prejudice. But it's sad. Coach isn't fifty yet, but it was like old age, maybe Alzheimer's, was thickening around him like fog." I couldn't mention that I was worried about Dad's head, too.

An antique convertible like one my dad had owned when it was new drifted along the county road. We were quiet for a moment.

"Something the matter?" Siiri asked.

"Oh no. It's just that when I see an old car . . . Dad and I used to take rides in his Buick into the country, along roads where the kudzu covers everything that holds still. It was so beautiful, like green snow over bushes and branches. Then some-one ruined it by telling me how kudzu kills the trees. I think that they are trying to control it with goats now."

"You miss home."

"Anyway," I continued, "I hung out with a friend named Kyle quite a bit. He disappeared during Katrina, or just after. A lot of people evacuated and never returned. His parents were meth-heads and lived in a shack up north of Baton Rouge. His dad just threw him out one day, out onto a shell road. So Kyle developed some problems, like that cutting yourself thing. His arms were a mess. Then he got really crazy. I think he had violent episodes, but I was too confused to help him . . . It was awful and I'm ashamed. But I did get a text message from another old friend."

After the Floods

"It must have been chocked full of news," Siiri said, flashing a wide grin that reminded me of Genevieve, another old New Orleans pal who worked in Marie Laveau's voodoo shop in the Quarter.

"It just said *yo*."

"Cryptic. Well, maybe he was on the freeway. I'm not a big cell-phone person. Someone said that hell is other people, but to me it's other people on cell phones. Anyway, I'm sorry that some of those you care about aren't well." She put a hand on my arm.

"Thank you. The one I care about up here is okay."

"Communication . . . ," she mused.

There was something on her mind, but I didn't ask.

"Are you coming back to the tundra, Bill? Think wood ticks and canoes. Think Friday Fish Fries by Lake Dakota. Think Swedish meatballs in the evening and lefsa in the morning. Lemonade at noon. And do you know what it means to miss pork and beans?" She was at once playful and earnest. "Oh, and think blizzards. We mustn't forget our blizzards."

"Yes. I mean, I miss New Orleans—the litter, the panhandlers, the transvestites, the mammoth cockroaches. But I want to come back here . . . eventually." Then I looked out into the trees that Sandy had taught me to name. "I . . . don't have the right words today," I said, flooded by feelings.

"Okay, tomorrow will be good. How old are you, Bill?" She fingered her bubble-gum wrapper self-consciously, and then slowly turned those miracle eyes my way.

"Twenty-five. Why?"

"Oh, just doing the math."

"A calculating woman?"

"Hmmm. Bubble gum?" she asked, offering a package.

"Sure, I'll try most things twice. And where's Sandy's dad?"

Billy in the Shade

"I'll describe that train wreck another time, and you can tell me about your New Orleans life."

Sandy returned from his puppy check and flipped me the football.

"Lemme see your spiral," he said.

I sent him out for a long one near the fence, where his bicycle rested nose up by a fallen branch. Sandy caught the ball over his shoulder like Jerry Rice, dropped it, and turned.

Raising both arms to the sky, he shouted, "Touchdown!"

"Super catch, Sandman!" I called to him across the lawn.

Sandy pumped his fist and bowed, knelt to retrieve the ball, and trotted in for hugs and refreshments, zig-zagging to kick as many leaves as possible. The trees beyond the fence moved slowly among themselves. They had their own world and didn't care about ours. The whisper of the wind was not a voice but only a sound, and the distant clouds, moving serenely to the east, carried no messages. I was home, and our team was on its own. Only a single crow in a tree looked at us with anything like interest. It was a good feeling.

"Mom! I bet that's the biggest bubble you've done since sixth grade!" When the bubble collapsed on Siiri's nose, we erupted in a trio of laughter.

"Well watch this," I challenged. "I can pop a bubble all over my face. Always could!"

"That's nothin'!" Sandy replied. "Gimme some gum. I can blow a bubble with my whole head inside!"

"Oh yeah? Well I . . ."

"Boys!" Siiri shouted, grabbing our hands, "Boys! Order in the court!" Her laughter sparkled like a sun-drenched river, and Sandy and I were happy swimmers.

After the Floods

A Declaration of Independence

To: Sister Ann
From: Billy
CC: The World
Re: Freedom now

Hi Sis,

I dreamed about you the other night, or about the you I imagine. This is a you who has two children of around 10 and 4 years. You work at a radio station, and in the dream the earth was about to open and swallow your town, but the station could not get the message out because the transmitter was down. You and the others were trying to think of ways to help. Your children were with you because the school had closed, and they wanted to tell you something but they had lost their voices.

The weird thing was, I was aware of myself as the dreamer and I wanted to make the dream better for you, but I couldn't change it. Sorry. It was like waking life, where sometimes I see myself from someplace else, like there's a second me watching in the shadows or from branches like that crow. Anyway, hope you don't believe the bad stuff in the dream was wish fulfillment.

Maybe we're just God's bad dream, and He can't change it although He wants to. I wrote this letter to God yesterday, but He isn't reading His mail. I decided to send it to you so you'll know how I've changed. I decided not to capitalize His name anymore just show Him, but I just noticed that I'm doing it again here. Maybe He needs sympathy instead of scolding. Anyway, here's the letter:

I've been hard on you, god, and this isn't an apology. You are off the team, at least for now. But most of Us believe in second chances, so you go somewhere and think about it. Take a nice booze cruise to Andromeda. Travel first class. Bring the wife. If you decide to change, if you can grow up a little and be a more responsible god, and a friendlier one, We'll be ready to give you another look and a conditional contract. If you're thinking about another flood, it'll only be knee-deep. You better supply toy arks for the kids, and no letting your children be nailed up on crosses. That really sucked.

We don't relish the thought of you being lonely out there in space. But you need to realize that your attitudes aren't working for Us these days. You have people-skills issues. There are three stages you need to go through: first, recognize your mistakes; second, seek forgiveness; third, learn to laugh at yourself. Then, if you decide to come back, understand that We'll write the Second New Covenant next time. Take it or leave it, because We're tired of living in your bad dream.

Oh, and you need new gear. Lose that silly robe. Is there a Goodwill up there? Also, a new hair stylist might brighten up your attitude. Maybe some tanning? A manicure? Spend a few bucks! I'm just trying to help. Image matters. Just ask Renaldo.

Enjoy your rest.

Well, Sis, I don't think I'll sign on for another three months with you, either. Not right now. It was silly to ask you for tips on being myself, but I was pretty insecure. Things are better now. It must be frustrating for you to try to help people and then not know what comes of it, so I want you to know that you've been a big help. It was certainly worth $75, and I know you probably need the extra cash, what with those little mouths to feed.

After the Floods

I'm going back to New Orleans for a while to see how Dad is doing, and the whole city, too. That means my email pal will be Siiri. It has been wonderful being with her and Sandy, sitting in the shade of her maple with lemonade and bubble gum. I hope that the shade in New Orleans won't be too dark, and I hope that Siiri and I get back together. But it's strange how things drift and change.

Your friend, Billy

Branchings

Smoky, Come Home

Smoky had come back to the levee often since Kyle's death, but now he was finished with the river. One of the dogs had told him it was a big worm. It smelled like dead things, and the other strays who gathered along the levee were a committee of curmudgeons, lying in the grass yapping and yipping at one another and the world. It had been weeks since the faculty of speech had left them, drifting off like mist in the night to wherever such things go. But the levee gang seemed not to know it. They seemed to think that each yip, yap, or woof carried deep implications for the future of the planet. *Dumb as a box of kittens,* Smoky thought. *I'm out of there.*

So Smoky wandered up Dublin Avenue, sniffing again the spot where Kyle had died and glancing up at the stairs from hell. Clouds ambled in from the gulf. When the afternoon rain arrived, a soggy Smoky crept under the awning of a small porch attached to a yellow shotgun house. Eventually the door opened a crack, its chain lock still in place, and he saw part of a woman's head, its gray hair tumbling like mist across an eye.

"Are you a good dog?"

She had a crackly voice, like a bag of biscuits being opened. Not a bad thing, her sound, but it was tiresome how everyone worried about whether you were a good dog. *No, I'm a great dog!*

After the Floods

Smoky wanted to say. Speaking had been cool, but those days were gone. So he gave the trusty old tail-wag that always seemed to set humans at ease.

"Okay, then," the woman said.

Her door closed, and Smoky heard the chain fall. Then the door swung open and the old lady stepped out on the porch.

"Do you have a home?" the woman asked.

She was a small person in an old-lady dress with pictures of flowers. She wore fuzzy house slippers. Smoky sat on his haunches and performed the gaze that follows the wag and completes the job of softening human hearts.

"You look so lonesome, and I bet you're hungry, too. You come in, then, and we'll see what's in the refrigerator."

He paused inside the doorway to sniff the mail on the floor. He had forgotten about mail slots and their mysterious way of delivering a daily and delightful bouquet of scents. In the kitchen, the woman removed something large from the refrigerator, peeled away the aluminum foil, and sliced some pieces of ham that she placed on a cracked plate. She bent slowly and placed it on the floor, steadying herself with a fragile hand on the counter. As Smoky made fast work of the ham, the woman drew water into an orange cereal bowl and repeated the slow process of stooping to the floor.

"There," she said, "that will be your water bowl." Then she picked up a plate that was covered by a towel. "Let's go into the living room and meet my friend."

Smoky followed the old lady to where she seated herself on an old sofa. The sofa was torn in places, and the cushion where the woman sat was concave from use. Her body sunk back into the mammoth flowers printed on the fabric.

Branchings

"This is my friend Miriam," the woman said. "Would you like a cookie, Miriam?"

The woman removed the towel from the plate, which did indeed hold cookies, and offered the plate to the air beside her. *Now that's special!* Smoky thought. The invisible Andy had been a problem. Nights of screaming stuck in Smoky's memory like shards of glass. And now Miriam? *I'm out of here.*

But then the lady picked up a cookie and held it toward him. Her hand was as delicate as an egg shell, and her fingers were translucent. Smoky eyed the veins nervously, and then took the cookie. *Peanut butter!* He gobbled it quickly and looked up expectantly as the old lady talked to the air beside her. *Maybe,* he thought, *I'll be out of here when the cookies are gone.*

Smoky listened as the old lady explained to the place in the air called Miriam that her grandson visits often because her daughter is a single mother and must work. Although he could no longer speak, Smoky remembered enough words to understand some of what was said. He did not know "autistic," but he did understand that the old woman had heard that dogs make good friends for children like her grandson.

"You will make him calm and happy," she said, smiling down at Smoky.

Then she offered a cup of tea to the air. Apparently the air accepted, and the old woman poured tea that was also air into a cup that was air. Smoky might have been spooked had he not had the Kyle/Andy experience, but now he watched the lady's pantomime with amusement.

"What's that? His name?" the woman asked the air. "I just don't know. I'll need to give him a name. Now let me see . . . Fritz! We'll name him Fritz! Here Fritz! Here's a cookie!"

After the Floods

Smoky took the cookie and weighed the cons and the pros. Fritz sucked. It really sucked. But then what are the chances of finding a human who decides to name you Smoky again? A stray has to go through the naming ordeal. It's the hand you're dealt.

The lady was nuts. Her head was a tree full of birds, and there would be an ongoing problem about whether Smoky was sitting on or in Miriam. But on the other paw the lady seemed kind, and an imaginary Miriam would mean more cookies left for Smoky. Ham followed by peanut butter cookies added up to a very large plus, an excellent way to jump-start a relationship. And there were no cats to scratch your nose. The prospect was brightening.

No doubt it would come down to the grandson. *Is he a good boy?* Smoky wanted to ask. It would be nice to help a boy with issues, and Smoky would help if the boy didn't hit him or pull his tail. He knew the advantages of being friendly to humans. "No tail pulling," he tried to say, but all that came out was a whimper.

"Can you sit up, Fritz?" the lady asked, extending another cookie.

Well, here goes. Smoky got his front legs under him and gave her the old, familiar look, the one that makes them think they're gods.

At Claudia's

It had been Daryl's idea to wear matching blue, Kat's blue being a cashmere sweater by Marni and his a Van Heusen shirt under a black leather jacket. Although they wanted to arrive early at Jenny's party (there was another to go to later in the Garden

Branchings

District), they paused by the door of the gallery to inspect Carl's largest photo one more time. At one end of a park bench in the photo, a smiling old man in an overcoat clutched a bottle, and at the other end a young couple gazed at one another, the man kneeling as though to propose. In the background a child danced in the grass.

To the extent that a pretense was needed, the party at Jenny's would be for Carl, whom no one had seen since Katrina. Now he was back in New Orleans, and his photographs proudly adorned the walls at Claudia's, one of the better galleries on Royal Street. Daryl wanted Carl to know that they'd taken his work seriously, and he thought it would be fun to invent an interpretation of the largest picture.

Kat had prowled different streets when Carl lived in New Orleans, but Daryl had elevated her lifestyle. Recently, they had spent five days in New York seeing plays and visiting museums. She had wandered among faces embalmed in ornate frames at the Frick, had sat on benches at The Cloisters, and leaned over railings at the Guggenheim, all the while vacillating between screaming boredom and exhilaration at being a well-dressed lady taking in the arts. On the whole, it was worth her while to entertain Daryl's whims.

"Here's the thing, Kat. It's like the bench in the picture is time," he said, arranging his words like a poker hand and assuming the thoughtful manner that had brought so many adventurous girls streaming to his office at Tulane. "To the left you have the young people in love. Notice how way yesterday they are. Their gear is nineteen-fifties. That girl's dress is vintage *Leave It to Beaver*. In contrast, the old drunk at the other end is today. Time moves to the right, right? The picture invites us to meditate on the emptiness of the bench in between."

After the Floods

"Cool," Kat agreed, playing the pretty, doe-eyed co-ed. "You know so much! Maybe the drunk is dreaming about the young couple. I mean, like, they *are* his dream. That's why he is smiling. Am I on the right track, Dr. Weaver?"

"Well, actually he *was* the young man," Daryl explained, enjoying the co-operative improvisation. "The couple is the drunk's dream about himself when he was in love with a willing damsel. It's a reverie of lost love viewed through a bottle."

"Why the heavy coat?"

The role playing was ending, and Kat was happy to let it go. Sometimes Daryl's imaginative flights reminded her of the days when she was the slut behind the bar trying to calm Kyle with his imaginary, ponytailed friend. Those were the days when Kyle also thought he could talk to that dog that smelled like road kill. Kat wanted to keep imaginings to a minimum.

"I don't know," Daryl replied, pushing up the sleeve of his leather jacket to check his watch. "The coat must fit in with the time thing somehow. He doesn't know what season it is? There's silence in every tale. Anyway, I think class is about over."

"Well, the old man drank too much and lost the girl. Let that be a warning."

Sometimes Kat surprised herself at how proper she had become since hooking her life to Daryl's that night in the Maple Leaf Bar. She had decided a year ago to change, to molt, and now her clothing by Marni announced her success. To soften the criticism of Daryl's drinking, since he had been her meal ticket, she smiled and gave him a playful nudge. The nudge didn't take, and Daryl felt a rush of annoyance, a small rush like caffeine kicking in. In the last few days, such references and warnings had become a motif in Kat's song.

Even as Kat had moderated her own drinking, there had

been a flood of hangovers for Daryl, hangovers medicated by the occasional morning joint or lude. And there were always parties in New Orleans. Just the past week they had been up to their necks in the John Guidry's scotch, the McCormacks' martinis, and the LaRoccas' bourbon.

"You know how you get," she added, dropping the pretense of playfulness.

"Oh fuck, Kat . . ."

"Don't oh-fuck me. You know."

"No, I don't know."

"You're in denial. You're becoming the old man in the photo."

"Grow up. I'm getting into publishing, and I need to meet people. When you meet people, you have a drink. I'm not going to teach Introduction to Shithouse Graffiti at Tulane for the rest of my life."

"I don't want to find you in the hallway again with that Reed woman draped around you like a snake in a freak show." She gazed through the door toward the coat-check room as she spoke. "I won't be treated that way."

"It was just a party. It didn't mean anything. Grow up, Kat."

"You run along. I'll stay here until they throw me out." She stepped away, and then turned to face him again. "Maybe I'll meet you later. Try to stay sober."

"You can't miss Carl's party. We need to stay together."

The whine of his voice annoyed her, as it always did. He could be such a child, such a goddamned three-year-old. She was tired of Daryl and his arty friends. Their big event of the week was writing a letter to the editor, and their endless talk made as much sense as snoring. Suddenly she wanted an all-nighter at The Leaf. She wanted to dress like a slut, get hit on, and fuck a stranger in the storage room.

After the Floods

"Appearances matter to you, don't they?" she said.

"Oh fuck . . ."

"Carl's picture was staged. It isn't reality. This is reality."

"What the hell does that mean?" Daryl grumbled.

She didn't know what it meant, but she had learned Daryl's trick of cryptic superiority. She shook her head, the blade of her annoyance sliding back into its sheath.

"You run along, Daryl."

Daryl stepped onto the sidewalk, dodging an elderly couple who had paused at Claudia's window, which he managed not to glance at as he moved toward Canal Street. Two young men in tank tops smirked at one another on the corner, and a man and woman leaned on a balcony rail, sipping drinks and watching the foot traffic below.

It was the week of Jazz Fest, and New Orleans was well supplied with tourists looking for a taste of Sin City, almost as many as in the old days. There would be a crowd on Bourbon Street, and Daryl decided he'd duck over there for a drink or two before Jenny's party. He had civilized Kat, had helped her to cultivate her tastes. She'd come around. And if she didn't, well . . . it would be just another knife in the heart. In the meantime, you never knew what adventure you might wander into on Bourbon Street.

Going Away

For all of his life Tony, Billy's father, had loved to travel. Now he sits motionless by the window, looking out at the new crepe myrtle that his son planted for him a few weeks ago. A squirrel scavenges beneath its branches, and further off on a power line

Branchings

a solitary crow surveys the street. It is late afternoon. By leaning forward, Tony can look to his right and see the beginning of Audubon Park, where he and Billy had walked their dogs, first Dusty and later Tim. He remembers the many ducks in the pond, and then he remembers the day that Dusty died so unexpectedly on the sofa in the house on Chestnut Street.

There are a suitcase and three boxes by the door. The crying is over, and it is time to go. He waits, wishing that he could go away another way.

Then he remembers the family visits of his childhood in the Forties. His father was back from the war, where he had been a surgeon. The family was together again in the large house on St. Charles Avenue, and other relatives visited often. As ceiling fans turned languidly, the aunts and uncles would sit in the shuttered rooms, their hands clutching coffee cups brought by the black maid, their eyes moving across dusty windowsills and picture frames, dusty tables and walls.

Each of these afternoons, it seemed to him then, was a dream vanishing slowly like air from an old tire, until finally, finally, the aunts and uncles would go away as rain drifts down a street and out of sight. Maybe these afternoons, endless and dull, had made him yearn for travel.

Now, even with his son back from the North, the old man dreams of travel again. He remembers the old Buick and imagines the thump of tires on a road winding through a valley. *I'll drive alone at dawn,* he thinks, *along a bending river, and I'll stop at diners in the towns where farmers come to talk. I'll smell the skunk a stray dog chased, and I'll rest where minnows glide like fingers through a creek.*

He longs to lie down by a bay and hear the ocean breathe as pelicans patrol the swell and pipers pick the water's edge.

After the Floods

And then at night the stars will tell of bones the sea tossed far and wide—a lover lost, a brother drowned, an old man shipwrecked in the tide. His knows that his longing could be a poem.

He wants to write his thoughts, and his hand moves toward the table but then falls still as a telephone rings in the next room. The old man looks at the clock that stares back at him silently from among pictures and pottery on a shelf. In the old days clocks ticked, and he had always loved the sound of a clock nicking away at the hours and days. He hates the silent, stealthy clocks that have crept into his life.

Now Billy stands in front of his father.

"We'll stay here tonight, Pop, and make the move tomorrow. The staff has clean-up issues at the home. We can watch the Cubs on TV and drink a beer. We'll have a good old time."

"Then you'll go back to that woman in Minnesota. You'll go back to live by Lake Lickapoo."

"Dad . . ."

For a moment, Billy imagines the obscene catastrophe of gray faces and bodies slumped in wheelchairs down endless halls.

"Lake Lickapoo!" the old man taunts. "Lickapoo Joy Juice!"

Tony falls silent, as he always does after an outburst. Tomorrow he will continue to go away, gathering into himself as the sea does when the tide ebbs, as rivers do when the flood is over.

The Statue and the Oak

Ruby Corvus rests on a low arching branch of a live oak in Audubon Park. Across St. Charles Avenue, Touchdown Jesus stands on the lawn in front of Loyola University, gazing into the autumn sky. The statue reminds Ruby of the winged person

Branchings

in the cemetery where she had spoken to the mist. Today the clouds above the Jesus statue whisper to her. They look liked crushed pearls. Closer by, bikers and joggers orbit the park, and closer still a man and a girl sit by the pond near the golf course. A few feet from them, a boy tears pieces from a loaf of French bread and side-arms them into the pond.

"So this is it?" the girl asks, her voice green and shaped like a leaf or a heart.

The girl's peasant skirt is tight around her knees, and a battered copy of *The Branch Will Not Break* lies in the grass beside her. Ruby cocks her head to read the title. The man, in jeans and a polo shirt, reclines on an elbow and contemplates the golfers across the pond.

"I guess so," he replies.

"And what about me?" the girl asks, her voice rising. "What will I do?"

A chocolate Labrador wanders along the bank of the pond, looking for another tree. His black leash is a snake trailing among acorns and pebbles. In the water, a family of ducks follows the bread splashing among clumps of Spanish moss that have drifted down from the oaks. Ruby sighs, tired from her lonely flight back from Minnesota. *The world is full of broken branches and of broken bridges,* she thinks, *the broken bridges of our dreams.*

The man abandons the golfers and turns to the girl. "You'll graduate," he says. "You'll become old."

The girl looks at her watch, and then she tells him that this will be the moment when she began to hate him. She tells him that her hatred will be fire. Her eyes are small spoonfuls of autumn, and they make Ruby hear wind in lonely trees.

The boy moves further away from the couple, flings the last of

After the Floods

the bread into the pond, and turns toward home, pausing at the bike path. He waits for open spaces in the traffic, imagining that they will be stepping stones in a rapid stream. Car horns debate on the avenue, and further off a bronze butterfly shimmers on the shoulder of Touchdown Jesus. The afternoon has begun its slow glissando into evening.

The girl walks away along the pond, but the man remains sitting. Ruby gazes off toward the statue as a breeze lifts the butterfly from its shoulder. *Strange,* she thinks, *the drift of things. So strange.* She sighs as a bird might sigh at the memory of a wandering hawk who had soared down to her out of the crevices of the sky one day when she was young.

River of Dreams

Jeffrey and Sandy

I suppose once someone like Birdella May has kicked time out of whack, and ten years of growth have washed themselves into three weeks in July, it'll take a while until life seems normal again. And when it does, it will be a different sort of normal. So when the following spring rolled around, turning the skating rink into mud and Lake Dakota back into water, we were still getting used to being special, to hearing our go-getters boast of creating the Rodeo Drive of the North or the Champs Elysees of the Midwest.

The new university splashed out theories, students, and controversies. Gopher learned to use the scissors and kissed the spittoons goodbye, Fred got into landscaping, and Homer now ran Homer's Home Accessories. The renamed newspaper, Seth called it the *Cold Beak Beacon*, supplemented the local news with opinions about movie stars and rock stars.

You never know where progress will take you, and I'm glad my mayoring days are over. There's too much now for one old coot to keep an eye on. Nightlife has evolved in the nurturing caverns of clubs and saloons on the north end of Prosperity Boulevard (no more Main Street for us). Rappers with genuine prison records and a language all their own play Cold Beak. Last month Danny Hell was here to rave reviews, causing more than one citizen to wonder where Ferguson is when you need him. What they call

After the Floods

progress can drag an eerie shadow behind it. Anyway, in the fall our first annual Moon Dance Film Festival will garner the planet's attention, which I'm not so sure that we need.

But in the meantime, school kids like Jeffery Lund and Sandy Elden have to make it to the June finish line.

• • •

Mr. Nygen turned, wiped his nose with a checkered sleeve, and leaned back against the blackboard to chat about what he'd just demonstrated with chalk marks. When he returned to the board, half of his dusty illustration had been transferred to the back of his shirt. *A styling guy*, Jeffery thought. It was sixth hour, and Jeffery had had enough of school. But there were twenty minutes to go, and Mr. Nygen, Cold Beak's last chalk-and-blackboard teacher, was getting revved up about sound waves. The children were young, but he wanted them to know that sound is particles of air bumping along.

"That's how your thoughts migrate to other people. Little collisions in the air."

Finally science class clattered to an end with shuffling papers, dropped books, and scraping chairs, all the collisions of busting loose.

Jeffery, banking and arcing through traffic, took his bike to the park by the river, the Gerald Lund Memorial Park, recently named in honor of his father. He let his bike down gently on its side, stretched his own body out in the grass, and closed his eyes to listen more intently to the bird songs. It was a time to be by himself.

Then, in a dream, he prepared to play his blue violin in an auditorium raucous with monkeys. His bow began to glide upon the strings. Slowly the noise left the room and flowed into the

River of Dreams

violin, which became heavy with the sound that had filled it. Jeffrey swayed in an ecstasy of utter silence, of the music of nothing. The monkeys continued to try to chatter, but the blue violin absorbed the sound before it could be heard.

"How can you just go to sleep like that?" It was Sandy, letting his bike clatter to the ground beside Jeffery's. "Don't the ants get on you?"

"Skill," Jeffrey said, opening his eyes. "Mom says I'm a sleep machine. I just dreamed that I was playing a blue violin, only the music was silence. You played the violin and all the noise around you was sucked into it. It was a backwards thing."

"Why blue?"

"That's just what color it was," Jeffery said.

"Who wants to make silence?" Sandy asked.

"Me."

"I just thought of something," Sandy said. "What if you only took away parts of the noise so that what remained wasn't noise but something beautiful? It would be like sculpture when they chip away marble to create the shape. You could call it sculpted music and it would be a new thing and you'd be famous for a while."

"Cool," Jeffrey said, his mind elsewhere. "Is your mom going to marry that guy who came back from New Orleans?"

"They're talking it over. He's renting a cabin out on Lake Dakota, but he's at the house all the time. I like him."

"Cool," Jeffery said again, looking out over the river.

"Maybe your mom will find you the perfect stepdad."

"I don't want a stepdad."

"I'm stupid. Sorry."

Jeffery closed his eyes. "I'm playing my violin," he said. "You need to be quiet now."

After the Floods

Couples

I liked Siiri Elden, Sandy's mom, the few times I talked to her, although some people call her the village atheist. Elvira Emerson is especially strident. The man that Siiri was planning a future with turned out to be the one we'd called Alligator the previous summer. He had been on vacation up here, and occasionally at the B.S. we'd say hello. You may remember that I mentioned him before.

We still call it the B.S., by the way, even though Gopher has gussied things up and now refers to his "styling salon." He's got some knew ideas about the hair biz, something about combining the salon with a coffee shop, and he dreams of owning a national franchise.

Anyway, no one knew much about Gator, except that he wasn't really from Atlanta as Gopher had claimed. We liked him fine, but we didn't miss him when he left. Now he was back. It's always a surprise to learn that life has been churning along unobserved just outside of your headlights, and the Elden-Alligator connection was something new to talk about if you got tired of discussing the prices of land or dreaming up new building projects. Everyone is talking business and investments in Cold Beak, and sometimes it seems that the heart and its softer negotiations are drowned in the babble.

So I'll stick to finishing an inventory of those who snuggle. Pete and Mattie, who had come to Cold Beak from their respective places of damage, built themselves a new house just below the hill from the Borguson Institute. It has levels and angles, balconies and towers, like something in a story book made out of cake and ice cream. It happened because Mattie invested in the Institute and got rich. Pete is now the Director of Parks and

River of Dreams

Recreation, with an assistant and a computer that he's learning to use. So they're doing well, and Hulda tells me that they're planning a trip to Europe.

Elvira Emerson was heard at the beauty shop to complain that Mattie and Pete were living in sin—fornicating like rabbits, I think she said. I trust that talk like that is in its dotage in our town and will soon be put to rest. Rev. Olson and her husband started the funeral by driving out to fairyland to visit the couple, giving their tacit approval to bunny love. Maybe God has lightened up on some of those old issues. I wouldn't mind.

Homer and Betty are doing fine, and Birdie and Oscar just helped Oscar II to dock on our shores, weighing in at ten and a half pounds and screaming to break glass. I lost track of the young girl and her Clydesdale. I believe they've moved away, as the young will do, but I have faith that his pecs are still hard and that her new boobs keep her afloat in romantic waters. I'm sure other young hearts beat in the old, moonlit way in Cold Beak. I hope they do.

Old Willy Berg, Hulda's dad, is in the new nursing home overlooking the New Hope River, and Hulda is okay. I don't think she intends to marry again anytime soon. When I imagine her followed down the street in the rain by the whisper of her lost husband, it rains in my heart too.

Then and Now

I've lived in Cold Beak all of my life, except for a side trip to Vietnam in the Sixties compliments of Lyndon Johnson and his generation of fools. I was born in 1941, just before Pearl Harbor and America's entry into WWII. My grandfather had been in

After the Floods

WWI, and I still have a Memorial Day (they called it Decoration Day then) photo of the two us in front of the old Dutch Colonial house. I look to be about three—little Lars Johnson. Grandpa is stiff and somber in his uniform, and I am standing beside him on the wide wooden arm of a lawn chair, wearing my sailor hat at a jaunty angle. My uncle was in the Navy.

My dad was absent from the get-go. According to my grandfather, he was a useless man hardly worth damning. According to Mom, he never met a barmaid he could resist. I guess he was a lot like Mattie's ex. Mom worked various shifts as a nurse in St. Paul, visiting Cold Beak when she could.

We had a maple tree in the front yard, and in back an old chestnut tree struggled on from year to year. I'd lie by the tree rocking in a hammock strung on a metal frame, and I'd imagine that I felt like the ocean feels, rocking in its own vast place. Mom, home on a day off, would sit in the grass under the tree and read one of the many adventures in Oz to me. I have a photograph of the two of us out there.

My grandmother, her name was Lillian but we called her Nana, is always old in my memory, battling weeds on her knees in the garden, marching me to church on Sundays, or coming to the children on the lawn with cookies in the evening, her clothing rustling like leaves. Everyone in town had lilacs then, and they were the purple smell of early summer evenings. Roofs sported lightening rods but had not felt the prod of TV antennas, and the only satellite was the moon. The sound of evening was crickets and owls.

As shadows thickened under the Dutch elms that reached out to touch one another across the gravel road, we'd sit on lawn chairs and listen to the neighbor's German shepherd, tethered

River of Dreams

to a post, evoke the failing light with his repertoire of yips, howls, and whines. Eventually, as a breeze sighed contentedly, Nana would tell a family story, pausing to return the waves from cars crunching along the road. Granddad often joked that her memory was so powerful she could recall things whether they'd happened or not.

Maybe the little slice of Cold Beak history that I gave you earlier, my story about Birdie and Pete and everyone, is an extension of my grandmother's voice and of those summer evenings that have disappeared beyond the wind. I know there are important things that are only owned by those who remember them, things that keep trying to disappear in yesterday's shrubbery.

In the late Forties, there was no concrete swimming pool with all the chlorine you could drink, so on summer afternoons some of the kids would gather at a swimming hole in the creek out across from the New Hope River. This was before the Barton Memorial Bridge was built, and you'd ride your bike across an old, nameless structure. What did an old bridge need with a name? As you crossed it, you were certain that one day you, your friends, and a lot of loose lumber would all tumble down and wash up on shore somewhere in Iowa if not Oz. It was strange to think of the road and the river crossing each other, so different and so alike.

My friend, Lyle, and I stopped on the bridge one day to watch the river falling upon itself in the sun, showing its teeth and calling to us in a strange language, as the road did sometimes as well. There was something the river wanted to say as it rushed on, lonely in its knowing that we couldn't understand. Maybe God is lonely like that, too. Anyway, the water wanted us, we thought.

After the Floods

It is strange how distances call to you, and yet it is this place and this landscape that defines you, even though much of it changes. The old bridge held up for the duration of our childhood, although it did fall eventually, snapping like a branch and spilling many workers and two cars into the river. Some died, and then the Barton Memorial replaced it. Destruction and creation are locked forever in their tango.

Anyway, Lyle and I always made it across the old bridge to hide our bikes behind tamaracks a mile down the road and walk our secret path out to the creek, the branches above us shuffling their green cards.

The swimming hole was out by the area where the Sowers eventually settled, but in my day it was just trees and countryside, blackbirds and crows. A wooded hill bulged in the distance, and we always talked about going there one day, trekking through fields under hobo clouds that rode the west wind. But we only splashed about in the creek, sending the frogs and shiners scurrying amid pulsing blotches of sunlight, and then we sat on the bank, our flesh turned to Braille by the icy water.

You'd warm slowly as the sun reached through the trees to fling gold coins on the creek and the birds carried on their endless discussions in the branches. Perhaps a garden snake would slip through the grass beside you like the thread you had pulled from your sweater and were scolded for. Once, when it was only two of us at the swimming hole, a butterfly floated by on a leaf that had curled up at the edges, a hand holding its delicate rider. It was like something from a book my mother had read to me. We didn't know then that they were our best days flowing away.

And we might talk about the future, Lyle and I—about what we thought it was. Years later, Lyle died in Vietnam. I found his

River of Dreams

name on the memorial, and others I'd known too, when I went to Washington a few years ago, the names of boys who swim in creeks in no one's memory now, all these decades down the river.

So things were different when I was a kid, or else we saw and heard different things. Kids listened to The Shadow and Sergeant Preston on the radio and read Dick Tracy in the Sunday paper. We went to Sunday school and learned that *darn* was a swear word. Adults bought war bonds, and if they didn't drive a Chevy they drove a Ford. The river never flooded, and the soil was rich. But, like Jeffrey's father, some from our parents' generation didn't come home from their war either.

I miss those old days. I'm not saying change is bad, although some of it is. We could have done without the Sowers in Cold Beak and without the warmongers in Washington. I don't expect America to climb back over Eden's green wall, but why are we kicking the fallen world into ever darker holes?

As far as our little town is concerned, I'm certainly not saying Pete and Ole shouldn't have renovated that old fried chicken place and allowed Birdella May to alter the fabric of time. That's not what I'm saying. It's just that a creative deed like Birdie's will have consequences that are many and endless, and those consequences move you further and further from the home you knew, as do the destructive deeds of benighted zealots wherever you find them, in the woods across the river or in Washington— leaders so monumental in their own minds and so much less in reality than even their own shadows at noon.

They wrench us further from home, and yet, when I see Sandy and Jeffrey by the river, their bikes in the grass, and I think about Lyle and me . . . well, then I realize that lives then and now are not so different, that it is all the same river.

I remember my first home, though, on summer evenings

209

After the Floods

when a thousand old moments come up out of the fields like insects or seeds to blow across the lawn of my present home. There were trees then where it's only buildings now, trees that would turn and swell in the wind after a rain. We were at the edge of town, and out behind Nana's garden we kept a field with horses. Nothing is prettier in the morning than horses in a field.

It is odd, the things that memory brings back in its partial way, a world in thin pieces—the cookies on the front lawn, the rhubarb you stole from a neighbor's garden, the day you got *The Wizard of Oz*. You just remember a few of the ripples, not the whole the river. I don't know any writers, but I think that's what all stories are about, the ripples moving away down some vast river, and the words we find to describe those moments are in the river too, swirling together and then apart.

• • •

Birdie and Oscar had a few of us out to dinner the other night. Oscar II is only six weeks old, and it was my first opportunity to shake his hand and welcome him aboard. Actually, he shook my finger. Pete and Mattie were there, as were Homer and Betty. And of course Ole showed up with Swede, the only girl for him. I was the token old guy, and I came alone. I lost someone a long time back, and things have stayed that way.

We sat on lawn chairs as the afternoon deepened toward evening. A flock of crows settled like soot on Oscar's shed. A moment later one crow seemed to bark orders, and they all exploded into the sky, leaving our patch of it to the swallows, who swooped and darted after gnats. The cattle slouched back toward the barn.

Oscar and Birdie have neighbors now, thanks to the expansion

River of Dreams

of the town, and from across a field we could hear the voices of children playing Marco Polo. We played hide-and-seek in my day, but the principle is the same. The principle is timeless, and as the evening star came to life over the trees, the kids' voices made me think of the girl I had sought and found as a child and then married. She's like a star in my mind, her light coming to me down the years.

The day fell softly, like a leaf, amid the talk and the laughter. We heard all about Homer and Betty's great adventure in Florida's spring-training season. Birdie laughed at something Oscar had said, and then others laughed, their voices flaring like fireflies. Homer chewed gum. More stars began to spot the darkening sky one drop at a time, and we went inside.

After enjoying Birdie's vegetarian hot dish, we said goodbye to Oscar II, who lay in a bed with a pacifier plugged in his mouth. I think he smiled. Birdie and Oscar waved from the porch, and our cars caravanned to The Phoenix, where the neon sign was still blue and the older crowd still danced.

Fred was there, but I didn't notice his fly. Perhaps they broke up. With Swede dozing at our feet and the trophy deer staring out from their plaques, Ole and I listened to the young bartender expound on investment strategies as the three couples, our friends, circled the dance floor. I believe that Mattie sang gently into Pete's ear:

"Warm as the month of May it was,
   And I'll say it was grand—
   Grand to be alive . . . ."

Pretty soon Siiri Elden, Sheriff Maki's sister, showed up with Alligator, and the small waitress from The Brown Ungulate arrived with her guy. Everyone talked to everyone else. We all

After the Floods

agreed that the old music is the best, and that's what they danced to. The dancers moving among one another made a living tapestry, just as our lives do. Later we sat on the patio, listening to the river whisper its song and its dream to the northern lights. A year had whispered its song to us, too, and then rolled on.

About Lost Hills Books

Lost Hills Books is a small press established in 2007 in Duluth, Minnesota. It publishes literary fiction and poetry, and submissions are by invitation only. Lost Hills begins with two publications: the novel that you hold in your hands, and a collection of poems entitled *From the Other World: Poems in Memory of James Wright.*

James Wright was a towering figure in American literature during the last half of the previous century. Wright's poetry represents his quest for an ecstatic union with nature, a quest repeatedly thwarted by the brutalities of industrialism and urbanization. Challenging America to define its values, his poems assert a sense of brotherhood with society's outsiders—the criminals, vagabonds, and the working poor who populate America's underclass.

From the Other World contains elegies and tributes from many of Wright's contemporaries, among them David Budbill, Robert Bly, Richard Hugo, Galway Kinnell, W.S. Merwin, Stanley Plumly, Gibbons Ruark, C.K. Williams, and Sander Zulauf. These poems are gathered together for the first time in *From the Other World*, and they offer valuable insights into the relationships among America's finest poets of recent decades. Interspersed with these are other poems by a newer generation of writers influenced by James Wright's work.